LOVE ON THE TRACK

By: Alithea-Jea Smith

Love On The Track
SBinkley Publishing, LLC
Alithea-Jae Smith
All Rights Reserved.
Copyright © 2016 by Alithea-Jae Smith
This eBook is licensed for your personal enjoyment only. This eBook may not be re-sold or
given away to other people. If you would like to share this book with another person, please
purchase an additional copy for each person. If you're reading this book and did not purchase it,
or it was not purchased for your use only, then return it and purchase your own copy. Thank you
for respecting the hard work of this author.

This is a work of fiction. The events and characters described herein are imaginary and are
not intended to refer to specific places or living persons. The opinions expressed in this
manuscript are solely the opinions of the author and do not represent the opinions or thoughts of
the publisher. The author has represented and warranted full ownership and/or legal right to
publish all the materials in this book.

This book may not be reproduced, transmitted, or stored in whole or in part by any means,
including graphic, electronic, or mechanical without the express written consent of the publisher
except in the case of brief quotations embodied in critical articles and reviews.

Editor: Jasmine B (Pixie Styx Editing)
Book Cover: Aija Butler
Formatting by: Sheena Binkley
Published in the United States of America

"A man's gift makes room for him and brings him before the great."

Proverbs 18:16 (ESV)

I would like to thank God for blessing me with this beautiful gift of storytelling. This gift has no value without him. For that I'm forever grateful.

To my parents Lawrence Smith and the late Antoinette Smith, I say thank you. Daddy, thank you for believing in me when I didn't believe in myself and also telling me, *"I'm proud of you...."*

Mommy, your absent in body, but present in spirit. Thank you for your undying support and love, also passing on your go-getter spirit.

To my family and friends, thank you for your support and love and always being there for me even during my darkest hours.

Also, I would like say thank Te Russ and Sandra Ivy. Te thanks, for your motivating spirit and always being a listening ear from time to time. Sandra Ivy, you have become like an aunt to me. Thanks for your sweet and calm spirit and always willing and ready to give me advice.

Finally, I would like to thank my big sis, my mentor, and my friend Sheena Binkley. Our amazing friendship all started with two characters, Jay and Brit. Thank you for always having faith in my gift.

Love, the Diva with a Pen '

Alithea-Jea Smith

oxoxo

This story is dedicated to my mother, Antoinette Smith, and my sister, Unissa Pratt; my two best friends who are also my angels...

Prologue

Mrs. Munroe wrote on the blackboard, "When I grow up, I want to be a...." She then turned to her fourth grade class and explained that this would be the topic for today's Creative Writing lesson.

"Before we start writing, let's discuss some of your ideas."

She looked at the faces of the children as they excitedly raised their hands, signaling their desire to be the first to be called upon. She decided to pick on Kenyon first because she knew for a fact what he wanted to be.

"Kenyon, what would you like to be?" Mrs. Munroe asked. He took a minute to answer the question.

"I want to work with money and win an Olympic gold medal for The Bahamas, just like your husband, Sammy "The Bolt" Munroe," Kenyon responded to his teacher with excitement in his voice.

Mrs. Munroe simply smiled, feeling delighted. She remembered how Kenyon had told her he wanted to win an Olympic gold medal after watching her husband in the summer games. He went on to describe in great detail that he wanted to win a gold medal for the 200 and 400 meters. She knew deep down that Kenyon would achieve whatever goals he set for himself. That was just the type of passionate determination he had in him.

Mrs. Munroe moved around the class and listened to the other students as they listed their desired professions. Everything from doctors, lawyers, teachers, police officer, fireman, actors, singers, rappers, and basketball stars were given. She noticed that she had one student remaining.

Finally, she asked Lauryn, "Lauryn, what would you like to be when you grow up? Is it a doctor or a lawyer?"

The tiny fourth grader looked up at her teacher and said, "No, Mrs. Munroe." She smiled and said, "I want to win a gold medal, too, at the Olympics, and to be a writer." She also knew deep down that Lauryn would also achieve her goals, because despite the fact that she was small in size, she was also passionate.

"Okay class, now that we have talked about what we want to be when grow-up, I want you to take out your creative writing books and tell me why you chose to be a lawyer, doctor, etc."

Kenyon interrupted his teacher and said, "Also, Olympic Gold Medal Winners, Mrs. Munroe." She stopped and gave him a side look. Kenyon apologized for interrupting her, and she continued with her instructions.

Kenyon raised his hand and said, "Mrs. Munroe, I have a question."

She rolled her eyes at Kenyon; she already knew what his question was about. He wanted to know whether or not he had to do the assignment, because he knew that next week would be his last day of class before he moved to North Carolina with his mother in the New Year.

"Yes, Mr. Carter, before you ask, I already know the question, and my answer is yes, you do have to do your assignment. Just because you're moving, that doesn't mean class work stops."

Kenyon mumbled under his breath because he felt like he did not have to do any more class assignments before he left. She shook her head and looked around to make sure that everyone was doing their assignment. She noticed that Lauryn and Kenyon were cutting up with one another instead of doing the assignment. Kenyon had always had a crush on Lauryn, just as she had on him.

She smiled inwardly and closed her eyes as she said a silent prayer for her students, especially those two. She knew the depth of their passion and, most of all, their determination.

The bell rang and the class was dismissed for lunch. Kenyon watched Lauryn cross the playground as he quickly walked up behind her. As she got her lunch, he asked, "So, you want to win an Olympic gold medal just like me?"

Lauryn looked at him and made sure her face gave no expression while answering him. "Yeah. So what if you want to win an Olympic gold medal like me?"

Kenyon started to laugh at Lauryn, who he considered one of his best friends, but also biggest his biggest competitor.

"Okay, Lauryn, you want to be Miss Smarty Pants. We'll see who will make it to the Olympics first."

Lauryn stepped up to him with a serious face and boldness in her voice and said, "I will see you there, Kenyon."

Like a bat out of hell, she ran off to eat with her best friends, Renee and Mia. Kenyon just smiled and ran to play with his best friends, Tayshaun and Jonathan.

From that moment, Kenyon and Lauryn's passion to win a gold medal was born.

Chapter 1

Fifteen years later...

Kenyon walked into the home that he grew up in for the first eight years of his life, as well as where he spent every summer until he was fifteen. It still looked the same, for the most part. There were some minor changes, like the walls were no longer white; they were now tan. There were also more modern furniture and appliances, cherry wooden floors, and an extra bedroom had been added.

Nevertheless, everything was still the same in Kenyon's eyes. Kenyon knew if these walls could talk they would say something like, "If it hadn't been for your grandmother, Isadora, you, your brother, and your cousins would not have made it to your sixteenth birthdays." However, one thing was for sure: Grammy's cooking hadn't changed. Whatever she was cooking smelled damn good!

Kenyon made his way into the kitchen where he found his grandmother, along with three of his aunties, Yvette, Karen, and Bridgette, fixing a dish and gossiping. Kenyon cleared his throat to get the ladies' attention.

Isadora looked up and noticed it was her grandson. She quickly wiped her hands on the cloth that was on her shoulder. She smile and gave her grandson a hug. Isadora was seventy-seven, but she could easily pass for a woman in her early 60s. She was no more than five-feet-two inches tall, and her hair was long and gray, which she would usually wear up, but today it was braided down in a single ponytail.

"Look at my grandbaby, Champ, looking just like your granddaddy," Isadora said as she kissed her grandson on his cheek.

Kenyon was the carbon copy of his maternal grandfather, Robert "Bobby" Carter at his age. Kenyon stood at six-foot-one; he was made of pure muscle, had a smooth caramel complexion and deep brown eyes, and he had dreadlocks going down the middle of his back. Hearing his grandmother call him Champ made him feel like he was really at home. That was the nickname his grandfather had given him as a baby. He was born eight weeks early, weighting a little over two pounds. The doctor told his mother that he would have various complications since he was a premature baby. If anyone looked at him twenty-five years later, they wouldn't have known.

Kenyon leaned in and kissed his grandmother, whom he was more than happy to see. "Gram, you don't have to tell me twice that I am handsome; all the girls already do," he mentioned while giving each one of his aunties a kiss on their cheeks.

She smiled. "Just like all the men in this family, y'all full of y'all damn selves."

He smiled because he knew that was true. The Carter men were known for being self- centered at times, but they took care of their family.

"Dinner should be ready in about 20 minutes. I hope you're hungry; we cooked all of your favorites," Sonya said.

The one thing that made him happy about being at home, and made him do a happy dance, was that his grandmother, who had been taught to cook by her mother and grandmother at age seven, was still cooking the same way seventy years later. She had also taught her daughters. For some reason or another, the cooking gene had skipped his mother, Lisa, who is the youngest of all the children, including the girls. Thank God for his step father, Gavin. If it hadn't been for him, Kenyon's almost certain that they would have lived off of take-out.

Kenyon didn't have to ask; he already knew what they were cooking: Pea soup, peas and rice, macaroni, fish fry, crawfish, coleslaw, and for dessert, guava duff.

"Yes, I'm hungry."

He sneaked a piece of macaroni before making his way upstairs to his grandparents' bedroom where his grandfather was lying down. He lightly knocked on the door since it was closed.

"Coming in!" Kenyon turned the doorknob to the bedroom and saw his grandfather was laying down, reading the newspaper. "Hey, Daddy Bobby, how are you doing?"

Bobby looked over his glasses at his grandson and gave him sly smile. "I am just fine, Champ. How are you doing, son?"

He shrugged his shoulders. "I am doing okay, Daddy."

Kenyon looked at the man who was more like his father than his grandfather; that's why he called him Daddy Bobby. His grandfather taught him everything a father should teach his son: How to write his name, ride a bike, and how to tie a tie. Kenyon loved and looked up to his grandfather greatly, but he knew his grandfather was also a man of business. For close to fifty years, he has been at the helm of Carter Liquor. He started out with only one liquor store; now there were twenty throughout the Bahamas.

Bobby embraced his grandson with a manly hug. He pulled back and stared at him with a look of pride. Out of his thirty grandchildren and five great-grandchildren, Bobby loved them equally; however, he and Kenyon shared a special bond. Sometimes it was scary how much they looked alike. The two even shared the same birthday: February 4th. Just like his wife of fifty-nine years, Bobby looked good for his age. At eighty-two, he was in perfect health and still went into the office at least three times a week.

"When are you going to meet with Jimmy?" He asked his grandson as he resumed his position on the bed. Jimmy was a well-known coach in the Bahamas. His grandfather asking him about

Coach Jimmy made Kenyon realize why he was home, and that was to train for the World Games in Singapore next summer, then make it to the Olympics the following year in Sidney.

"In the morning, at 11 AM, and then I have to go and see Mr. Taylor from the Bahamas Athletic Association office about me representing the country at the World Games next summer," Kenyon said.

They talked for few more minutes until Bobby informed him when he was not on the track training, he would be working at the head office of Carter Liquor, putting his degree in Economics and Finance to good use. Also, he was going to allow him to stay at one of the apartments in their family complex, and told him how much he had to pay in rent. He was happy that he was getting to stay in one of the apartments so he could have a little privacy. Kenyon was not surprised, either, about working at the liquor company, because his grandfather always said, *"Idle hands are the work of the devil."* His Uncle Neil was currently running the company in which all of the siblings were board of directors, and all the grandchildren were shareholders in the multimillion dollar company.

They went downstairs to eat dinner, but by the time they made it down, the house was already filled with the rest of his family. The only people that were missing were his parents, his brother, and his sister. Kenyon was going to enjoy tonight because, as of tomorrow, he would have one mindset, and that was getting to Singapore and Sydney.

※※※

It was shortly after seven when Lauryn Smith finally made it home. She was both mentally and physically tired. All she wanted to do was take a long shower and get into her bed.

"Rae, baby, you look like hell," her mother, Angelica, said to her as she kicked off her black pumps and flopped down in the chair. Rae was her nickname, but was also her middle name.

"I know, Mummy. I spent my day in Parliament listening to a bunch of old heads arguing over whether gambling should be legal or not. The last time I checked, I'm supposed to be writing about sports and not about damn local government deciding whether gambling should be legal or not. Is Daddy home yet?"

Angelica just shook her head and listened as her daughter vented about her day. She worked at *Bahamas Times*, a local newspaper, as the Assistant Senior Sports Writer. She was the first woman to hold that post in the paper's '95 year history.

"Look at it this way: you get paid to do what you love, and that is writing. Your daddy went out to play dominoes at Uncle Tommy's."

Lauryn knew her mother was right about getting paid. Also, for as long as she could remember, her father played dominoes with his brothers every Thursday. Angelica went back to watching television and putting rollers in her hair.

Lauryn got up from the chair and went in the direction of the kitchen, "I am going to eat, take a long shower and go to bed."

Just as Lauryn walked into the kitchen, the telephone rang; she picked it up.

"Hello! Hello! Hello!"

She could hear someone on the other end just breathing. "Look, I don't have time for games." She said angrily.

"Rae, who was that on the telephone?" her mother shouted from the family room.

Pouring a glass of juice, Lauryn shouted back, "I don't know. Someone into playing games."

Lauryn went into the family room to eat her dinner and continue talking to her mother, who talked about her day. Her mother was a General Practitioner at both her private practice and government-run clinics.

Angelica looked over at her baby. She was still as beautiful, but the fire she once had was gone. She prayed that God would send someone to help her get that fire back. Angelica knew for a fact that Lauryn missed the track so much, that's why she took the job at *Bahamas Times* as a sport writer. She knew something must have happened to her, and that was the reason for her hanging up her sprints. Angelica was a firm believer that everything happened for a reason.

Chapter 2

Kenyon looked at his watch for the second time in five minutes. He arrived ten minutes early at the training site with a mix of emotions. He was excited, nervous, and fearful all at the same time. He didn't know what to expect, because for the last six years, his former trainer, Coach McKay, had been training him. Kenyon had some of his personal bests, setting both state and school records at North Carolina University in the 400 meters.

He took a deep breath and was about to call his best friend, Tayshaun, when Coach Jimmy Thompson's assistant, came out and told him that he would see him now.

"Right in here, Mr. Carter. Coach Jimmy will be with you in a minute." She said with a husky voice.

Tonia stood about five-foot-six inches tall, had a well-toned body, and short fire-red hair that would most definitely stand out in a crowd.

She flashed a million dollar smile as Kenyon gave her one in return. "Thank you."

Kenyon could tell that Tonia was checking him out. Yeah, she had an amazing body, cute face, and pretty smile, but he was not looking for anyone to date right now.

"You're welcome. Can I get you any water, tea, coffee, or juice?" she asked before leaving the office.

"No, thank you." He said while sitting up in his chair. He started to play with his hands and sucked on his tongue, which was a sign that he was very nervous. The phrase, *"Blood, Sweat, Tears on the Track,"* was going through his head as he tried to calm his nerves. He loved the phrase so much that he had it tattooed on his chest.

Kenyon took a quick second to look around the office at all the pictures of different athletes that Jimmy had trained throughout the years. Everyone from his idol Sammy "The Bolt" Munroe, to the Sands twins and Antoya Johnson, were displayed. Between the four, they had all won multiple medals at the Olympics and The World

Game. One athlete caught his attention, and that was Lauryn Smith. Kenyon remembered having a crush on her back when they were in primary school. He hadn't seen her since their early teens. Last he'd heard, she was in school in Texas, and she had hung up her sprints due to an injury. Kenyon was kind of shock about that because she was having her best season then.

Two minutes later, Jimmy Thompson came into the office. He shook Kenyon's hand before taking a seat behind the desk. Jimmy was about five-nine, coffee-complexion, with gray hair closely cropped to his head. He was wearing a red track suit and running shoes. "Good morning, Mr. Carter."

Kenyon stood and shook his hand before returning to his seat.

"Good morning, Mr. Thompson."

Jimmy put up his hands and said, "None of that Mr. Thompson crap; you can either call me Coach or Jimmy. It's up to you, Mr. Carter."

Kenyon nodded before responding, "Coach is fine by me, but I would prefer you call me Ken or Champ."

Jimmy leaned back in the chair, put his two legs on the desk, and studied the young man's face. He looked much younger in person than in recent pictures. "Ken is fine by me. Okay, let's get down to business, Mr. Car…"

Kenyon arched his eyebrow. "I mean Ken."

He smiled and said with confidence, "Basically I want you to train me for both The World Games and the Olympics, both of which are over the next two and a half years."

Jimmy put his feet down and sat up straight before answering. "Why do want me train you, Ken? I watched your tape reviews; they were excellent."

Kenyon gave a wide-eyed expression. "Why not, Coach? You're the best in the business. You've produced some of the best athletes that have ever represented the Bahamas; from the Caribbean Junior Games to the Olympics."

He pinched his nose and said, "I am the best in the business, so I have been told. I have been watching the tapes from your meets over the last four years. I must say, Coach McKay has done an excellent job with you. Your times are amazing, I'm not even going to lie."

Kenyon smiled. "Thanks, Coach. Coach McKay has played a big role in my track career so far, because he has been training me since my freshman year of high school, and I was blessed when I found out he was also going to be my college coach.

"I have been weighing my options for the last nine months, and I realized that Coach McKay has already done what he could with me. If I want to go to the next level, I know for a fact that only you can help me get there. The athletes you have trained are legendary, and I want to be legendary too," Kenyon said with confidence.

Jimmy took a deep breath. "Ken, you have so much in you, and I would be honored to train you. I am a man who doesn't like bull shitters, but bull shitters who want to work. We'll start tomorrow with some drill runs and tests.

"Oh, and don't worry about Mr. Taylor from the BAA office; I will deal with him. I already know he is going to try some dumb crap with you."

Kenyon trusted Jimmy enough to deal with Mr. Taylor. Besides, his grandfather knew Jimmy as well, since they were frat brothers; he knew he could be trusted.

Both men got up from their chairs, shook each other's hands, and said their good-byes. As Kenyon was walking out, Jimmy said to him, "Just remember, once you give your all, you will be legendary."

Kenyon looked at the man who was about to help him build his legacy. "I will remember that, Coach." Jimmy nodded as Kenyon left his office. Out of all of the athletes he trained, his mind wandered to one in particular: Lauryn Rae Smith. She once had the same passion for the sport. Jimmy didn't have any doubt that Kenyon would become legendary; he already knew that he would be.

❋❋❋

Kenyon was beyond happy because he had a coach to train him. All he had to do was work his ass off and win a gold medal.

As soon as he left, he called his mother, who started crying. He also called his step-father, who was just as excited as he was. He even called his grandparents and gave them the good news. He finally called Tayshaun, who told him that they were going out to celebrate tonight. Kenyon started laughing because everyone was damn happy that he got Jimmy Thompson to agree to train him.

✳✳✳

Lauryn sat in front of her boss, Editor Chief of *The Bahamas Times,* Drake Miller, as he informed her about the game plan for the next few weeks.

"Lauryn, just remember I need you to be on your A-game for the next couple of weeks because Kaylisa is out with a broken arm and will be unavailable for four weeks. You will be wearing several hats, including being the assistant editor, finishing up her article titled *Start up Business in the Bahamas,* while still doing your job as the sports writer.

"I also need some ideas for the special edition we're doing on the *Golden Girls* and *Golden Knights* in our August issue," he said while editing an article and sipping on his coffee.

Lauryn just sat there and looked at him as if he just told her that her daddy had passed. "Drake, are you for real?! Do you realize that I am a sports writer? You have fifteen other people who are capable of doing the jobs that you are asking me to do," Lauryn said angrily.

Drake looked at her with an *as-if-I-give-a-damn* expression.

"Yeah, I realize that you're the sports writer. So, if you don't have any other questions, don't you have layouts to finish? We have a deadline to go to the printer."

She sighed. Truly, she did not want the job because it was bad enough half of the office was talking about how she was sleeping with Drake. That was far from the truth. He graduated high school with her older brother, Ryan, so that made him about twelve years older than she was. One thing Lauryn didn't do was date anyone five years older than her. She hadn't dated anyone since her ex, Shannon, who had turned her world upside down.

Once Lauryn got back to her desk, her phone rang. She knew it either had to be Mia, Renee, or Jonathan. It was her twin brother, Jonathan; he was the oldest by two minutes. While Jonathan favored their father, who had an easy-going personality, Lauryn favored their mother, who had aggressive and stubborn personality.

"Rae, I need to use your car for the next couple of days."

Lauryn shook her head. *"No 'Good afternoon, Rae, How are you doing? Can I use your car for the next couple of days?'"*

"Good afternoon, Rae. How are you doing? Can I use your car for the next couple of days?" Johnathan repeated.

"First of all, what the hell happened to your car? And how in the hell am I supposed to get around?"

"My truck is getting a new paint job, and you can drive Angelica's car while she drives Quentin's car since he's still away in

Freeport for work," Jonathan said as he took a bite of his sandwich. He had always called their mother by her given name whenever he was referring to her in a conversation.

Lauryn went silent for a second. Jonathan thought she had hung up. "Yeah, you could use my car."

"Thank you and love you, baby sister. I have to go because my lovely girl Kai is waiting on me to bring her lunch."

Lauryn rolled her eyes. She was not surprised when he talked about taking Kai to lunch. She wasn't a fan of Kai because she had a very nasty attitude, along with being a gold-digger in the making.

Over the last five years, Jonathan was so timid and only cared about computers and planes; now he's this confident and sexy pilot who's definitely not shy about the opposite sex.

"Yeah, I love you too," she said before hanging up.

Over the next four hours, Lauryn finished up her layout for the paper and got a jump start on some of Kaylisa's work. By that time, most of the staff had already left for the evening. During that time, her cell phone rang. Every time she picked it up, the person would hang up. To make matters even worse, they were calling from a private number. She made a mental note that if the person kept calling her, she was going to tell Tayshaun, who was one of her best friends and was like a brother to her. He was also a police officer.

She picked up her phone and read Tayshaun's text:

Tayshaun: "Rae, I don't want hear any story on why you can't come by the Stadium to have a few drinks with Renee, Mia, Johnny, and myself. So see you there in the next half hour. And don't even try to skip out, either."

Rae: "I don't care what you say, Tay, I'm going home to my bed."

Tayshaun: "See you in one hour, baby sis."

Lauryn grabbed her bags and headed downstairs to her car. She started cursing under her breath because she really wanted to go home and watch the basketball game in her favorite big t-shirt. She didn't want to go out for drinks with her friends.

She sighed, deciding that she would go for thirty minutes.

Chapter 3

Half an hour later, Lauryn was walking into The Stadium Sports Bar and Grill; it was Lauryn and her friends' favorite spot. Whenever their crazy schedules allowed it, that would be the first place to go. It was no surprise that they all had demanding careers: Renée was a nurse at the hospital working out of Accident and Emergency, both Mia and Tayshaun were police detectives, and Jonathan worked for the National Fly Carrier Air Bahamas as a pilot. He was also a volunteer fireman during his spare time.

Even on a Wednesday night, The Stadium was packed; all six of the pool tables were in use. The bar area was filled with men who were talking about local and intentional sports, along with trash talk about the government. All the tables were mostly filled on both the inside and on the deck outside.

She noticed Renée and Mia sitting at their usual table. She was already upset because she didn't see Tayshaun and Jonathan, which only meant that they were late. That wasn't a big surprise; the only place they were ever on time was work.

"Hi ladies," Lauryn said while taking a seat next to Mia.

"Hi Rae," both ladies said.

Lauryn noticed four empty beer bottles. She knew right then that it was going to be a long night. It was a proving fact that both Renée and Mia couldn't hold their liquor. Lauryn picked up a bottle and said, "I see you ladies have got the party started." They all laughed.

Mia was the first to speak." What do you expect us to do when y'all never on time, especially the boys."

Lauryn nodded as she grabbed a Buffalo wing. Wings and coffee were her weakness.

"Okay, girls. Tay just messaged me and said they're on their way. Oh, and Rae, he has a surprise for you." Renée said and gave a bright smile.

Lauryn stopped chewing and looked at Renée." You damn well know I hate surprises. I don't know what y'all up to, but whatever it is, stop it now, she said, pointing at both of her friends.

Renée gave an innocent glance. "Rea, truth be told, I don't know what's going on."

Mia took another sip of her beer before she answered. "Rae, my hands are clean. You know that I am always the last to know what's going on."

All three of them started to laugh at Mia's statement because it was the truth. Mia was the smartest of them all, as she graduated from high school as the class's valedictorian. She was able to pull off both a Bachelor's and Master's, all before her 24th birthday, and still found time to become a detective.

"That's the God's honest truth, Mia. To be honest, I don't have any idea what the surprise is. Besides, we all know that you hate surprises," Renée stated.

"I don't give a shit what it is. I know one thing for sure, though; if any harm is done, you won't have a baby daddy, Renée, Lauryn said. Renée only smiled because she knew that Lauryn was dead serious.

They talked for another twenty minutes before the guys arrived. Lauryn was the first to notice them. She saw this young man coming behind Tayshaun, and he looked exactly like Kenyon Carter.

It can't be, Lauryn thought.

If it was him, he was definitely fine. When he got closer, she realized it was him. A funny feeling came over her; she suddenly had butterflies in her stomach. It was like she was eight years old again and they were back in the fourth grade. He clearly wasn't a fourth grader anymore. He had definitely grown up and was fine with it.

Kenyon's eyes locked with Lauryn's as they gave each other longing stares. Kenyon quickly thought that Lauryn was prettier than he remembered. She looked much younger than twenty-four.

"Sorry we're late, ladies, but you have to blame Playboy Jonathan. Oh, and surprise, Rae," Tayshaun said as he brushed a kiss on Renee's lips. He then blew air kisses to Mia and Rae.

Jonathan rolled his eyes at Tayshaun. "Blame it on Tayshaun, ladies."

Lauryn was somewhat surprised to see Kenyon. She knew, thanks to Kim from the BAA offices, he was home training for the World Games and the Olympics. She often kept in the loop of what was going on in the Association. She wasn't expecting to see him this soon, though, but she should have known that he would been hanging out with both Tayshaun and Jonathan; they were his best friends, after all.

Tayshaun stuck his middle finger up at Jonathan. "Ladies, you remember Kenyon." All three of them nodded in agreement as Jonathan called the waitress to bring around some shots.

The waitress returned with six shot glasses filled to the rim. Tayshaun raised his glass. "This shot is for my boy, Kenyon 'Champ' Carter, who is officially home training for the World Games and the Olympics. To Kenyon and his gold medals."

Everyone raised their glasses and threw their shots back.

Renée asked Lauryn to move down so Tayshaun could sit next to her. She wanted to slap those two for being in love. When she sat next to Kenyon, she could feel him looking at her with those chocolate eyes of his. She thought he was so fine with his five o'clock shadowed beard and jet black dreads that rested on his shoulders.

She was so nervous that she took a long sip of her drink. Lauryn knew if she didn't slow down with the vodka that she was going to make a fool of herself with Kenyon in attendance.

Kenyon could tell that Lauryn was totally uncomfortable with him looking at her, but actually found it rather cute. He studied her face, seeing that she looked the same as she did when they were in primary school, but more mature. She could easily pass for someone in her late teens. She definitely kept her body right, her rich-brown complexion glowed under the bar lights. She put her fingers through her hair, which was brown and naturally curly, but with a hint of gold.

What really stood out were those big brown eyes of hers. He'd always loved them because they could light up any room, but now they were dimmed and distanced.

"So, Kenyon, who is your coach while you're at home training?" Renée asked.

Kenyon finished his drink before answering. "I am training with Jimmy Thompson."

Renée looked dead at Rae. "Oh really! Jimmy is training you. You know he was Rae's coach during her entire track career," she said happily.

Kenyon knew Jimmy was once her coach after seeing her picture in his office. "Oh, okay, excellent."

Lauryn forced a smile. "Yeah, Jimmy was my coach when I ran track. Don't worry, you're in good hands. Just don't be a little bitch, because he will work your ass off," she said and smiled.

She wanted to kill Renée Beatrice Sands. Why in the hell would she bring up the fact that Jimmy trained her when she ran? That's part of her life that she didn't want to acknowledge. It felt just like yesterday when she came home from Texas and told Jimmy, who played one of the biggest roles in her track career, that she no longer wanted to run track. She sat silently while thinking about that very moment.

"Rae has gone quiet on us," Renée said softly.

Lauryn looked around the table and saw that everyone was staring at her. "Oh, I am so sorry," she said with shame. Kenyon took another sip of beer and realized it was time to switch the subject.

He turned his attention to Mia first. "Mia, what have been up to?"

She smiled. "Well, I work with Taysahun in DEU and CSI." Kenyon glanced at Lauryn before turning his attention back to Mia

"That's good for you, Mia," he said. He was kind of shocked to hear that she was a police detective, especially because she was a former beauty queen. He turned his attention to Renée, who was sharing a light kiss with Tayshaun.

"So Renee, Tayshaun tells me you're a RN?"

She smiled. "Yeah, but I'm going off to specialize. Most likely in the next year or so. Lord knows I need a break from school," she said before giving Tayshaun another kiss.

"Damn, Ren and Tay, y'all need a damn room. Every time I look up, you two are kissing. I'm shocked there aren't no little Rens or Tays running around," Jonathan said as he put the finishing touches on his food.

Everyone started laughing because Jonathan was serious with his statement. Lauryn knew her brother was right; she was also surprised, since the two were always kissing or touching each other. But she was happy for her two friends, which came as a shock to everyone. They were enemies at one point where they both cursed each other out every time they were in the same room. Next thing everyone knew, they were going to prom together and then they were a couple. That was six years ago, and they were still together and madly in love.

Renee stuck her tongue out at Jonathan while Tayshaun gave the middle finger again.

"I love you, Tayshaun," Jonathan said in a girly voice.

Tayshaun pointed his finger at Jonathan while giving a wide-eyed expression to Lauryn. "Rae, your brother likes men."

Lauryn laughed as Kenyon looked on. For the first time that night, he noticed that Lauryn was relaxed. She has the sexiest laugh that he had ever heard. He thought everything was sexy about her: The way she talked, smiled, and sipped her drink, and even the way she looked at him when she thought he wasn't looking. He also noticed that she kept staring at the tattoo on his wrist.

He leaned over and whispered in her ear, "Kennedy-Makayla is my baby sister. She's 18 years younger than I am."

Lauryn gave a tiny smile as Kenyon gave her a wide one. He knew that she assumed that Kennedy-Makayla was his daughter. He acted like she was his daughter because of the age difference between them. He even named her Kennedy after him, and Makayla after his step-brother, Malik.

"Yeah, I know she could be my daughter," he said quietly.

"I guess you get that often?" she whispered.

He nodded. "I do, but I don't mind. She really is like my daughter because my brother, Malik, and I nagged my mom for a baby sister."

"Malik?" she asked.

"I have a brother named Malik, but he is really my step-brother."

"Oh, because I knew when we were in primary school you said that you were the only child."

He took another sip of his beer. "So you remembered?"

She smiled. Truthfully, Lauryn remembered everything about him, right down to the fact that he was left handed.

The group stayed for another hour; they had a few more drinks and shared a couple more laughs. They also talked about the dumb crap they did so Kenyon could hear the stories of their childhood. It was a fact that Lauryn was the peacemaker; Tayshaun was the protector; Renée was the sassy one and the mother figure; Jonathan was the wild child; and Mia was the one everyone took care of.

Kenyon stared into those big brown eyes that he had fallen in love with when he was in the fourth grade. He wondered why Lauryn had hung up her track shoes. Only time would tell.

Shortly after eleven, Mia yawed for the third time in less than a minute. "Mia, girl, you're twenty-four and you still can't hang," Jonathan said as he grabbed her hand.

As they were all walking to their cars, Lauryn and Kenyon walked a few step behind everyone.

"It was nice to see you again, Kenyon."

He smiled at the woman who was beautiful in every sense of the word. "Same here. I hope we get to do it again real soon, Lauryn."

She looked up at him and smiled. "Me too, Kenyon."

Kenyon held her against the passenger side of her car. He leaned in and gave her a kiss on the lips.

Lauryn was speechless. Even though the kiss lasted for a quick second, she was able to experience how soft his lips were.

Kenyon studied her face, wondering why she wasn't showing any emotion. He realized maybe it was a mistake to kiss her.

"I-I am sor-ry, Lauryn," he stammered.

Lauryn put her hands on his cheek. "There is nothing to be sorry for, Kenyon," she whispered.

He gave her a wide smile. "I will see you later, Beauty," he whispered.

Lauryn smiled and shook her head. She got inside of the car and leaned back against the seat while closing her eyes.

Jonathan looked at his sister before putting the car in drive. He continued to stare as she took a deep breath. She couldn't stop thinking about that kiss.

Damn, that was a kiss!

She knew she would been lying if she said she didn't feel anything when he kissed her. She was still trying to put the pieces together; she had not seen or even heard from Kenyon in fifteen years, but all the feelings she had for him were quickly coming back.

For a split second she thought about the time she spent with Shannon, then remembered she made a promise to herself to never fall hard for any guy ever again.

***

Kenyon was restless most of the night. He glanced at the clock and realized it was six in the morning. He knew he had a big day ahead of him, and three hours of sleep was not enough. He looked to the ceiling and his mind immediately went to Lauryn. She was gorgeous and had the sexiest lips he had ever seen. Her hair even smelled like his favorite fruit: peaches. He took a deep breath and swung his legs out of bed, heading straight to the bathroom. Since he couldn't sleep, he decided he should go for an early morning run so he could try to get his mind off of Lauryn.

Chapter 4

Lauryn sipped her morning coffee, feeling beyond tired and nursing a minor hangover. If anything, she was more tired than hungover. She spent most of the night thinking about Kenyon. She couldn't stop thinking about his walk, his voice, or those lips of his as she imagined him kissing her. She most definitely felt something between them last night even before they shared that kiss. The feelings were similar to the ones she felt back in primary school for him.

She sat back for a quick second and tried to recall if she had the same feelings for Shannon when she first met him. Even when they started getting serious about dating each other and started sleeping with each other, her feelings were not even remotely close to what she was feeling for Kenyon. She took another sip of her coffee and said out loud, "It's only *lust.*"

Lauryn quickly got it together, placed all of her thoughts for Kenyon at the back of her mind, and got started with the mountain of work she had to do. An hour later, her desk phone rang.

"Bahamas Times, this is Lauryn Smith speaking. How may I help you?"

"You can help me by telling me why you allowed Kenyon to kiss you," Renée asked.

"Renée Beatrice Sands, that is none of your business," Lauryn said as she cradled the phone to her ear.

Renée didn't say anything; she knew Lauryn was definitely feeling him if she allowed him to kiss her. "Fine, be like that, Rae. Anyway, Champ is not the reason why I am calling. I am calling to tell you that I ran into Shannon."

The mention of his name made Lauryn's body go cold. The last time she checked, he was still in Texas living with his girlfriend and rehabbing after damaging his ACL. So what was he doing home? She nervously shivered. "What do you mean you ran into Shannon?" .

Renee didn't say anything for few seconds. "What in the hell do you think I mean? When I came out of the hair salon, I heard this person call out my name. When I looked around to see who it was, it was Shannon. He told me that he was back at home and looking to train with Coach Johnson for the World Games. Then he asked about you, of course, so I lied to him."

"That doesn't make any sense. He just had surgery on both of his ACLs six months ago."

"He doesn't look like anyone who just had major surgery," Renée said.

Lauryn took a deep breath and started to count to ten before speaking. "Thanks for the heads up. Don't tell anyone else about seeing him, Ren."

"Of course not, Rae. I only told Mia, and you know she won't say anything."

"Thanks, Renee."

"Girl, please, we're sisters; just be careful. I'll call you later. Love you."

"Love you too," Lauryn replied and hung up the phone.

Her mind went to the first time she met Shannon. She had just turned fourteen, and he had just turned sixteen. It was the first track meet of the year. She'd just finished up her race, and Shannon was on the side of the track lacing up his sprints for his race when he stopped to tell her how good she looked out there.

"Mama, you looked nice out there. Oh yeah, by the way, I'm Shannon, and you're my girlfriend."

Lauryn just looked at him in shock, not knowing what to say. *"Thanks! I'm Lauryn, and you're not my boyfriend, Shannon."*

She started to walk off when he followed behind her *"Why not, Lauryn?"*

Lauryn stopped and looked at him. *"I am not your girlfriend yet because I don't know you."*

Shannon gave her a sly smile. *"Okay, cool, you got me there."* *He looked around with a smile and laughed.* *"So why don't you just give me your number so we could get to know each other* better?" He followed to get her cell phone from her gym bag. She handed it to him and he put his number in.

The rest was history...

"Stop daydreaming. Derek wants to see you," Lauryn's co-worker, Kelly, said and walked off to her desk.

"Okay, thanks, Kelly."

✳✳✳

Kenyon had just finished up practice for the day and was sitting on the track catching his breath. He did a half hour of warm-ups, two hours working out in the gym, and another three hours out on the track.

"You did well, Champ. At least you didn't bitch about it," Jimmy said while laughing

Kenyon took a long sip of his water and shook his head. "Thanks, Coach. I took your words to heart when you said that you don't take bitching too well."

Jimmy removed his glasses and replied, "You are a smart guy; that will get you far in my books. Hit the shower. I will see you here at the same time tomorrow."

"Yes, sir. See you tomorrow."

Kenyon headed towards the locker room as his mind went straight to Lauryn and that kiss they shared last night. Even though it was short lived, he could still taste her soft lips. He knew he wanted to taste those lips again, and soon. He thought that his ex-girlfriend, Ebony, could kiss, but damn, Lauryn was in a class all by herself.

He glanced at his phone, noticing that it was three o'clock. It was too late to ask her if she wanted to go to lunch, and it was too early to ask her if she wanted to go for dinner. He had to make a decision soon, but first, he needed to take a shower, then hit up Tayshaun for Lauryn's number.

❉❉❉

Lauryn stared in disbelief as she cradled the phone "No, he hasn't called. How in the hell do you know Kenyon kissed me last night?" Lauryn asked Mia while typing an article on the Gaming Act.

Mia laughed. "Do you have to ask? You know Tay and Johnny can't keep shit."

"Remind me to kill their asses later. Mia, baby, I know you don't have shit to do besides answer the phone, but I have an article to finish and five other edits all before 6 PM. So whenever I get home, I am going to call you."

Mia sucked her teeth. "Yeah, whatever, Rae," she said as Lauryn hung up the phone.

Twenty minutes later, the phone rang again. Lauryn knew for sure that it was Renée.

"Hello, Lauryn Smith. How may I help you?"

"Well, Miss Smith, you can help me by going out to dinner with me."

When she heard Kenyon's deep, sexy voice, a feeling came over her body, especially between her legs, which was foreign to her.

Even when she was with Shannon, she never had the same feeling, even after they started having sex.

"Rae, are you still there?"

"Oh, I'm sorry. What did you say?" she asked while trying to get her voice back to normal.

Kenyon smiled; he knew she was hot and bothered. He definitely was, too. "I said that you can help me by going to dinner with me tonight around seven."

Lauryn couldn't because she had a deadline to make. "Sorry, Ken. I can't go out with you tonight. I have a deadline to make by six."

Kenyon tried not to sound disappointed that he was rejected. "That's cool. Just give me a call and let me know when you're free."

He was about to hang up when an idea popped into his head. "Since you can't do dinner, why don't you come to the track with me in the morning to workout with me before you go to work?"

A shiver ran through Lauryn. She has not stepped on the track in eighteen months, and she wasn't planning to anytime soon.

Lauryn tried to find an excuse to get out of the invitation. "Champ, I don't think that would be a good idea for me to work out with you. I don't want to be a distraction to you."

Kenyon could tell from the sound of her voice that she was jittery. He remembered that she was the same way when he started to ask about Jimmy and training for the World Games. Something happened to Lauryn; that's why she was so nervous whenever someone talked about the track. He had a feeling her ex, Shannon, had something to with it. He knew then not to push the subject any further.

"That's okay, Rae. We could hang out some other time. I will let you get back to work."

"Thank you, Kenyon," she said, and then the phone went dead. Lauryn got up from behind her desk and went to the kitchen to get a glass of water. Lord knows she needed it. She had a lot of mixed emotions. She had no problem hanging out with Kenyon, as long it didn't have anything to do with being on the track.

She left the kitchen and went back to her desk to finish up her work. Lauryn's mind wandered to Shannon for the second time that day. She began to cry because she was angry at him, and at herself. She was more angry at herself because she'd allowed Shannon to take away her first love.

Chapter 5

Kenyon was four weeks into his training and quickly learning why Jimmy's training was legendary. Even though he was training six hours a day, six days a week, he knew it would pay off in the end.

Jimmy reminded him of his grandfather, Bobby, who was a hard ass, but was also down to earth. That was one of the main reasons he respected Jimmy so much. Kenyon also learned that Jimmy had raised four sons on his own after his wife, Belinda, died thirty years ago from breast cancer. It amazed Kenyon how he'd never remarried after all these years.

Kenyon may have been training hard, but that didn't stop him from thinking about Lauryn. Since that night when he invited her out to dinner, he had not spoken to her nor seen her. The few times he went out with Tayshaun and Jonathan, he'd been hoping he would get to see her, or that one of them would bring her up as a topic of conversation.

A few nights ago, while hanging out with Tayshaun and Renée, she had become the topic of conversation. Renée had simply implied that Lauryn was drowning herself in work. He didn't seem shocked, because when he called her, she did say she had a whole lot of deadlines to make. Kenyon just wanted to have the courage to ask about her. He especially wanted to talk with Jimmy about her because it seemed like he knew Lauryn from on the track.

Kenyon noticed a young man, who was well over six feet, coming over to where he and Jimmy were. Kenyon couldn't help but notice the displeased look on Jimmy's face as he watched the guy get closer.

"Who's that? Kenyon whispered.

Jimmy didn't take his eyes off of the man as he continued to walk towards them. "Champ, that's one really big jackass named Shannon." Kenyon wondered who in the hell this was; whoever he was, he could tell that Jimmy was not happy to see him.

He forced a smile as he shook Shannon's hand. "Shannon, I didn't know you were back on the island."

"Yes, Jimmy, I'm back training for the World Games," he said quickly, glancing over at Kenyon.

Jimmy looked over his shoulder. "Oh, Shannon, this is Kenyon 'Champ' Carter. He's also training for the World Games. Kenyon, this is Shannon Knowles."

As soon as Kenyon shook Shannon's hand, he got a vibe about him that he did not like. He immediately knew he was not to be trusted.

"Nice to meet you, Champ." For the first time ever, his nickname sounded distasteful coming out of Shannon's mouth. "I know your face from somewhere. Did you go to college in the Carolinas?"

Kenyon looked him up and down before answering. "Yeah, I went to North Carolina University. Where did you go to school?"

"I went to Texas University."

Kenyon's mind started to wonder if this character was Lauryn's ex, and if he was, the only thing he wanted to do was beat him to a bloody pulp.

Kenyon decided to play devil's first born and asked about Lauryn. "I had a friend who went to the same school as you. Her name is Lauryn, but most people call her Rae."

Kenyon didn't have to look at Jimmy to know that he was trying to figure out how in the hell he knew Lauryn. Kenyon never took his eyes off of Shannon.

Shannon didn't say anything. "Yeah, Rae is my ex-girlfriend. Why are you asking me about her?" he angrily asked. "We're getting back together."

Kenyon put his hands up and said, "Does she know that?"

"What do you mean, does she know?! Of course she knows, fool," he said with annoyance.

"Who in the hell are you calling a fool? Look, Shannon, you don't know me, so be careful what you call me, jackass."

"Hey! Hey! Watch y'all damn mouths. Kenyon, hit the shower, and Shannon, you need to go," Jimmy said.

"It was nice seeing you, Jimmy. Champ, I'll see you around," Shannon said and walked off.

When Jimmy was sure that he was gone, he turned to look at Kenyon. "Champ, how in the hell do you know Lauryn? Your ass only been here for three weeks."

"Actually, Lauryn and I went to primary school together. Her best friend, Renée, and my best friend, Tayshaun, are dating," he stated.

Jimmy arched his eyebrow. "I had to make sure, because Rae is my baby girl. That same jackass, Shannon, is the reason why I have time to train you. Eighteen months ago, she called it quits. On the blood of my four sons, I know that damn Shannon is the reason why she quit."

In Jimmy's eyes, Lauryn was more than an athlete he was training; she was the daughter that he never had. He knew Lauryn from when she was six years old, as she used to come out to the track on Saturdays with her older brother, Quentin. While he and his son, Jason, were doing their workouts, she would be doing it, too. Jimmy really didn't notice her ability until she was about eight. Like any other Saturday, she would be running up and down the track, but that particular Saturday, she started from the 100 meters. Jimmy's younger son, Xavier, decided to time Lauryn that day, and she clocked in at eleven seconds. Jimmy he was in disbelief with the time, so he asked Lauryn to do the 100 meters over. When she did, she clocked in at 10.98 seconds.

After that Saturday morning, he started training her. Lauryn became special when it came to the 100 meters and 200 meters. With the 200 meters being her event out of the two, she had the ability to run like no other. Jimmy still wondered how she did it with her height and size.

With Jimmy's coaching, Lauryn won 10 gold and 4 silver medals. In the Caribbean Junior Games in 2009, she set a record for the 100 and 200 meters. She also held the records for the 100 and 200 meters in both the summer games at the Junior American and Caribbean Championship in 2009, and in the 200 meters at the Junior Caribbean Athletics Games in 2010. She also held the 200 meters record at Texas University where she went to school.

"I didn't need a PH.D to realize that you held a lot of animosity towards Shannon."

"Hell yeah, because in the prime of her career, she dropped that bomb on me about quitting, and I know his ass had something to do with it. I know my child all too well."

Kenyon shook his head; he knew once he left the track that he needed find Tayshaun. Kenyon realized that Jimmy saw Lauryn as his daughter, so he would do whatever he could to protect her.

"I got you, Jimmy. Shannon is a real jackass."

"He sure is."

Kenyon got up and put his hand on Jimmy's shoulder. "Jimmy, I hate to tell you this, but I like your daughter."

Jimmy smiled at Kenyon. "You're telling this to the wrong man. I just hope you're daring enough to tell that shit to her actual father, Max Smith, who is the Commissioner of Police."

Kenyon laughed. "Yeah, I'm daring enough. See you tomorrow, Jimmy. I need to go and find Rae. Also, I have to get my ass to work."

"See you tomorrow, and don't rush up on her about Shannon, either."

"Yes, sir."

Kenyon showered and got dressed in record time. The minute he got in his truck, he knew he needed to talk to Tayshaun, and then to Lauryn.

***

Lauryn glanced at her watch and noticed she had twenty-five minutes left before she had to return from her lunch break. She parked her car and decided to walk to the jewelry store near her office. She needed to look for Mia's birthday gift since her birthday was in a couple of weeks. Lauryn loved the fact that her friends weren't hard to shop for because each one had their own fetch. Mia's fetch is jewelry, Renee's fetch is bags, and her fetch is shoes.

Lauryn was a regular at the jewelry store. It took her a minute to think because she remembered that she and Renee bought Mia a watch for her graduation gift, and earrings for Christmas. In the midst of her thoughts, she smelled a familiar cologne which reminded her of the one person she wanted to avoid: *Shannon*. She looked over her shoulder and saw that it was him. A state of panic came over her as she stood face-to-face with her ex. The last time she saw him was eighteen months ago when he was kicking her ass in her apartment.

Lauryn looked around but realized she couldn't hide from him anymore. Shannon looked and gave her that famous sly, evil smile.

He came over to her and whispered in her ear, "Don't cause a scene and let me walk you back to your office."

She nodded as Shannon held the door opened. When they got outside, he grabbed her hand as Lauryn quickly pulled it away.

"What in the hell do you want, Shannon?" Lauryn asked.

"I want you, baby. I don't like that you didn't tell your little friend, Champ, that we were getting back together."

Champ. Lauryn thought. She wondered where he talked to Kenyon and how Kenyon knew Shannon was her ex.

"For starters, we're not together, and when did you talk to Kenyon?" She asked.

As she waited for a response, Shannon looked around them and sighed. "I was looking for Jimmy today and Champ asked me if I knew you."

Lauryn arched her eyebrow in curiosity. She knew that Shannon and Jimmy never got along. "Why were you looking for Jimmy?"

"I was only stopping to say hello. As for Kenyon, I actually knew him because we went to school at North Carolina University."

Lauryn still had an uneasy look as Shannon gave another sigh. "Why are you looking at me like that?"

"Don't even ask me why, Shannon! You hate Jimmy, and I can tell you hate Ken without even knowing him. The last time I saw your ass, you were kicking my ass around in my apartment. And let's get something straight; this island is not that big, so make this the last time you come talk to me," she said in one breath.

"Rae, you are right; this island is not that big, so we will talk again," he said before walking off to his car.

Lauryn went straight to the ladies' room to get herself together before going back to the office. Once she did, she went to Derek's office, letting him know she would be taking the rest of the day off. She then grabbed her stuff and called Kenyon, but it was just her luck that his phone went to voicemail. She then called Renée to give her the rundown to what happened between her and Shannon. Renée later shared that Kenyon was working in the accounts department for his grandfather's liquor company.

Chapter 6

Lauryn arrived at Carter's Liquor in record time. She had a one track mind, and that was to give Kenyon a piece of her mind. She walked into the lobby and headed straight to the secretary desk. When she arrived, she was not too happy to see who was sitting behind it. Tiara Campbell, one of her high school classmates who she could not stand. All she could say to herself was, "Damn and double damn." In high school, Tiara was known as "Miss Busy Body," who was always in everyone's business. Also, she and Renée were foes.

"Hey, Rae, how are you?" Tiara asked.

Lauryn smiled. "Hey T. I'm doing fine, thank you. I'm looking for Kenyon Carter," she told her. Lauryn could tell by Tiara's facial expression that she knew Ken.

Tiara picked up the phone and called up to Kenyon's office. Lauryn looked around the lobby, noticing that Carter's Liquor was all about family and helping the community. Numerous awards from different organization were plastered throughout the office space as Lauryn looked at one.

. "Rae, Kenyon said you can come up. His office is on the second floor; go through the double glass door and you'll see his office on the right," she said while pointing towards the elevator. Lauryn got on the elevator, determined to tell Kenyon how she felt about him butting into her business. She hadn't seen Shannon in eighteen months, and all of a sudden, he popped up out of the blue. Then there was Kenyon, who she hadn't seen in fifteen years. The first night she saw him again, they kissed. After a month, she could still taste his lips and hear his soft sexy voice sounding like Keith Sweat.

Her thoughts became cloudy as she stepped off of the elevator and saw Kenyon was waiting for her.

The moment he saw her, he could tell she was frustrated; he could see it in her eyes. Despite the fact that she was angry at him, he couldn't help but notice how sexy she looked. That night at the bar, she looked younger than twenty-four due to her outfit. Today, she wore a simple black dress with a red narrow belt, a white blazer, the sexiest pair of black heels Kenyon had ever seen, pearl earrings, and a string necklace.

Lauryn's emotional state went from being frustrated to hot and bothered. Kenyon looked too good in a pair of black slacks and a pink shirt. That statement about only real men wearing pink was an understatement for Kenyon. The top button was unbuttoned, and his sleeves were rolled up. She also found that rather sexy, because it showed that he was a hard worker.

"Hey, Rae, this is a surprise to see you. Is everything all right?" he asked with concern.

"Hell no, everything is not alright. I'd rather we have this chat in private," she told him.

Kenyon knew, whatever it was, she was upset. "Sure. You're just in luck; my office mate, Ashanti, is out for the day."

Kenyon led her over to the chair by his desk. "Okay, Rae, talk to me. What's the matter?"

Lauryn took a deep breath. "The problem is you and my ex, Shannon, having a conversation about me."

Kenyon was not shocked at all that Lauryn didn't beat around the bush. That's one thing he always loved about her because she never was the one to hold back. But he had to wonder, how in the hell did she know about his conversation with Shannon? For what he gathered from Jimmy, they hadn't communicated in quite some time.

Kenyon had his index finger on his temple as his eyebrow arched. He studied her facial expression, which showed she wanted answers. Shannon is your ex?" He asked, trying to act surprise.

"Yes, he is my ex. Look, I don't have time for the damn games. Let's get something straight, Kenyon. Shannon and I have really bad blood between us. Shannon is the reason I'm living this damn nightmare each day of my life," Lauryn said as her voice started to rise. "As for you, Kenyon, you just pop up out of the blue after fifteen years, she continued, while tears fell down her cheeks.

"I have to go," she quickly said, getting up and walking towards the elevator.

Kenyon was shocked by what she just said.

What in hell did this guy do to her? He thought while walking to the elevator. By the time he got there, Lauryn was already gone.

"Damn," he said, hurrying to the parking lot. When he did, he saw only her back tail light leaving the lot.

✳✳✳

Lauryn was still crying, but she needed to get herself together, and fast. She knew she needed to go someplace to get her mind together. The only place she knew was at the track, but she quickly changed her mind. She glanced at her phone, noticing that Kenyon had called three times and left a voicemail. She decided to go straight home.

She sighed deeply when she saw all three of her brothers' cars were parked in the driveway.

"Just my damn luck these fools are at home," she mumbled as she got her purse from the backset.

***

Kenyon continued to dial Lauryn, cursing the entire time. He knew she was intentionally ignoring his calls, letting them go to voicemail instead. He knew that Lauryn was upset; that was one quality that Tayshaun warned him about. Her anger could be legendary in Tayshaun's opinion. Now, he starting to see why, too.

He rubbed his hand down his face in frustration; not only was Lauryn being stubborn, but she'd left his office upset. Lord knows that one of his biggest pet peeves. He never liked to see any female cry, especially her. He picked up the phone, dialed, after the fourth ring, Tay answered. "Good afternoon, Detective Thompson. How can I help you?"

"Tay, this is Ken. Where are you?"

Tayshaun knew it had something to with Lauryn. "I'm at work filling out some papers. So what went down between you and Rae?"

Kenyon explained to Tayshaun the incident that had transpired in his office earlier. Tayshaun listened, but cussed himself in his mind. He was also shocked that Shannon was back on the island. He wondered what the reason was for him to be back. Tayshaun hoped to his sweet Jesus that Shannon's plan was not to get back with Lauryn.

"Wow, I guess you got to meet the unpleasant side of Rae. Your best bet is just leave her alone for now; when Lauryn's upset, she fouls up. I mean, really fouls up. She doesn't want to talk to anyone, not even Renee and Mia. Let her come to you, which might be in a few hours, a day, or maybe next week. Who knows." Tayshaun told Kenyon.

"Well, all that is about to change, Tay, because fouling up won't help the situation. I don't give a shit if Rae's anger is legendary. My persuasion is also legendary," Kenyon said angrily.

"Clam down, brother man. If you feel like pushing the issue with Rae, by all means, go right ahead. Just remember that Rae's emotions usually affect Ren and Mia. If Renée gets upset with me because of you, I'm going to bust your ass." Tayshaun said.

Kenyon laughed. "I got you, brother. I will remember that. Anyway, Tay, I need to get out of here and go to the gym to get my mind right about Lauryn."

"Okay, brother, be safe," Tayshaun said, hanging up the phone. Tayshaun just shook his head; he knew once Kenyon put the pieces to the puzzle together about Lauryn and Shannon, he might be one best friend short, but that was the risk that he was willing to take.

❋❋❋

Lauryn walked into the house and started to mumble under her breath. Her brothers Ryan, Quentin, and Jonathan could always sense when something was up with her, especially her older brother, Que. The truth is, Lauryn has a special bond with each of her brothers. Being the only girl in the Smith house had its ups and downs.

Ryan, at thirty-seven, is the oldest. He's a project manager for the Ministry of Works, and he was the first of us to get married.

He and his long-time girlfriend, Lena, tied the knot early last year. They are now expecting their first child. He was a natural born leader, as his siblings looked up to him and often came to him for advice. Quentin is the second oldest; he is thirty-four and is a financial advisor for Bahamas Resorts. Que is the money man who seeks out financial issues and is greatly trusted when it comes to financial investments. Jonathan is the knowledgeable one who could debate any subject with anyone, while Lauryn was more of the mother, despite being the youngest. She could always hold her own with her brothers.

    She walked into the kitchen to find her brothers in their favorite places in the house. Ryan was looking in the pantry, Que was sitting on the countertop playing with his phone, and Jonathan was sipping on a beer and playing with his iPad.

    Ryan yelled, "What time is Angelica or Lauryn coming home?!"

    Lauryn threw her keys on the counter. "Why do you want to know when I'm coming home?"

Ryan turned around and started to laugh. "I asked because I am famished."

Lauryn shook her head; Ryan was always looking for food. "Don't you have a wife who cooks for you?" she asked while taking off her heels and jacket.

"I actually do have a wife who cooks for me, but I didn't have time to go to the store. Besides, I rather not be at home right now. Lena is eating me out of house and home, along with her different mood swings each day. That's why I'd rather have a home cooked meal by either you or Angelica. Thank you very much!" They often called their mother by her name when they were talking amongst themselves.

"How can Lena be eating you out of house and home? She's not even that far along in her pregnancy," Quentin asked his older brother.

"Well, Que, my brother, you're not the one who got her pregnant. One minute she's cussing me out because she has morning sickness, then ten minutes later I'm the best husband in the world," Ryan said as he put the finishing touches on his sandwich.

Lauryn looked at Ryan and smiled. She never thought that he would get married; his life was all about work, out of the blue, after more than ten years of being on and off, he and Lena decided to get married. Now they're going to be parents, which they're extreme excited for. She was truly happy for her brother.

"Oh, the joys of being happily married, and of impending parenthood, Ryan," Jonathan said smartly. Ryan threw a towel at his youngest brother.

Lauryn stood by the sink and looked out the window. Her mind was spinning from what had happened between her and Shannon, and also how she blew up at Kenyon. Well, more on how she blew up at Kenyon, but it served him right for having a conversation with Shannon about her. Even though she was mad at him, she couldn't help but notice how sexy Kenyon looked, and how calm he was with her. If that had been Shannon, he would have been trying to one-up her with his temper.

Her mind went back to the first time Shannon ever hit her. It was the weekend after hers and Jonathan's 16th birthday party. During most of the party, Shannon was upset with Lauryn, so he left the party early claiming he was sick. Over the next few days, she tried to call, text, and even email him, but he refused to answer her. It was that Friday when he came to pick her and Jonathan up from school when the incident happened. That Friday, Jonathan didn't go to school because he was sick, so it was only her going to school. Honestly, she was surprised that he came because they hadn't spoken since her party. When she hopped in the car, she leaned in to give him a kiss, but he turned his head. She asked him what was wrong, but he didn't reply; instead, he drove straight to the beach not far from her house where they always went to hangout. During the drive, his eyes had a fit of rage in them, which made her a bit scared. Once they arrived, he let her know what his problem was: that she had been dancing with different guys at her party. He felt disrespected and demanded an apology. At the time, Lauryn didn't think it was a big deal, which made her say he was acting like a giant ass. She realized that was a big mistake as Shannon swiftly slapped her across her face. So many emotions were going through her during that moment, from disbelief to anger to, most of all, fear. She started to cry and quickly jumped out of his car. He followed her, apologizing for his behavior and promising her that he would never hit her again. Lauryn quickly forgave him, but like the old people would say, "Promise is only conformed to a fool." That saying was so true. After that day, Shannon continued to abuse her physically and mentally until a year and a half ago when she put her foot down and decided to fight back.

She was still deep in thought when she heard her brothers calling her name. Quentin tapped her on the elbow to get her attention. "Lauryn, are you all right?"

"Yeah, I'm fine, Que. I was just thinking about something," she said to her brothers, who were all looking at her like she was on trial for murder.

"So you say, Rae. Anyway, why are you home so early from work? It's not even 4 o'clock yet," Jonathan asked as he glanced at his watch.

"I was not feeling well; my head was hurting, so I came home. I guess my monthly is coming soon," she said as she walked out of the kitchen towards the steps to her bedroom. Of course her brothers knew she was lying; she was a Davis & Smith woman. They held pain and drunk rum better than any man, so they knew something else was up.

***

Shannon was on his fourth gin and water in the last half hour. He wished he had slapped Lauryn right then and there for having such a sassy assed mouth. He threw back the gin and started thinking. He never wanted to hit Lauryn when they were together; however, she brought it on herself. His father, Shannon Sr., always told him the only way for a woman to respect a man was to hit her. He lived by that motto when it came to women. That was the only way he knew how to make sure a woman respect him, because that was the way his father dealt with his mother, Stacey. From time to time, he still slapped or punched her when she got out of line. Nevertheless, he was still in love with Lauryn; however, she never respected him, and that was the biggest issue they always had in their relationship.

This time around, her little ass is going to respect me....

Chapter 7

Kenyon left the office an hour early and headed over to the gym. He still felt a little frustrated with Lauryn because she was allowing her anger to get the best of her. He also had a feeling that Tayshaun was not being 100% with him about what had happened between Lauryn and Shannon. If his gut was right, Shannon was the reason why she came home eighteen months ago, and also the reason why she was no longer running track.

"Champ, is that you?!" his grandmother, Dora, shouted from the den. He could tell that she was watching South Florida's 5 o'clock news. As Kenyon made his way to den, he was surprised to see his three aunts, Bridgette, Karen, and Yvette, there. It was just his luck that his aunts would want to play 21 Questions, and he was not in the best mood.

"Good afternoon," Kenyon said while sitting on the edge of the chair arm.

"Afternoon, Champ," everyone said in unison.

He zoned in to the television while half listening to his aunties. He realized they were talking about his grandparents' upcoming party, which was in two weeks. He listened for another five minutes before excusing himself, with his grandmother letting him know that dinner was ready. The way Kenyon felt, he didn't have much of an appetite.

An hour later, Kenyon headed home and took a bath. He decided that he was going to turn in early tonight. It was an early night for his body, but his mind was a different story. He decided to play some video games, hoping it would get his mind off of Lauryn, but that was a lost cause.

He started to wonder what happened between Shannon and Lauryn. Did he cheat on her? Did he abuse her mentally or physically? Kenyon shook his head; Lauryn is too strong-willed for that. Besides, her brothers and Tayshaun were not sitting in Fox Hill for murder. What else could he possibly have done to her to make her have so much anger towards men in general?

He thought back to the night they went out for drinks. Her eyes always told her soul. Even when she was smiling, they had a hint of sadness in them. The way she acted today made him realize that he was right. His suspicions had been confirmed when Jimmy had become uneasy towards Shannon when popped up on the track today.

***

Lauryn was staring at the ceiling when she heard Jonathan enter her room. She turned on her side and pretended to be asleep.

He leaned over to her to see if she was awake. "Hey, Rae, are you awake? We need to talk about what's going on with you and why you're so upset."

She sucked her teeth before opening her eyes. "Damn, Jonathan, I can't sleep in peace."

"Calm down with the anger, baby girl. Just tell me what's going on," he said while getting in the bed next to her. Lauryn sat up and grabbed the remote control to change the channel. She was really not in the mood to deal with Jonathan.

Lauryn could not bring herself to tell him that Shannon was back on the island. She still could remember the expression on his face that night he came to the apartment. She saw nothing but pure hurt and pain, all because of what had happened.

She looked at her brother. "Look, Johnny, I'm about to tell you something, but you have to promise that you won't fly off of the handle."

Jonathan arched his eyebrow at his sister. "I promise, Rae."

She took a deep breath. "Shannon is back on the island. He came to see me today when I was coming back-,"

Jonathan put his hand up to interrupt her. "What do you mean, that son of a bitch is back on the island?! Did he come to see you?"

"When I was coming back from lunch, he was waiting on me nearby. By that time, he already had been to the track and talked with Jimmy and Kenyon. Then I went to Champ's job and tripped out on him for no reason."

Jonathan took a minute to calm down before speaking. "Listen, Rae, I want you to be careful. You know I'm out for blood with Shannon's ass. It's killing me every day not telling mommy or daddy what really happened between the two of you."

"I know, and I'm grateful that you have kept my secret from them, as well as Ryan and Que. I will be careful, but please don't tell Tay."

He took a long breath. "Of course. You know I will keep your secret, Lauryn."

She leaned over and give her brother a hug and a kiss. She hadn't been able to get through the last eighteen months without Jonathan. That night when she called him, she didn't have to tell him what happened because he already knew.

"Tell me what happened between you and Kenyon?"

For the next twenty minutes, she told Jonathan about the conversation she'd had with Kenyon. He shook his head and sighed. "You need to put on some clothes, jump in your car, and go tell

Kenyon you're sorry face-to-face. Do you even know why you went off on that boy?"

Lauryn smiled, knowing her brother would defend her in any situation, but when she was wrong, he would definitely call her out on it. "Okay, I going to apologize. Pass me my phone."

Once he did, she dialed Kenyon's number, but it went straight to voicemail.

Chapter 8

Kenyon quickly woke up from a deep slumber when he heard a knock at the door. The knock became louder as he slowly got out of his bed. It was clear the person wasn't going to let up. He glanced at the clock, seeing it was after 11. He groaned and made his way downstairs.

"This better be sweet baby Jesus at my door," he grumbled.

"Who is it?"

"It's Rae."

Kenyon quickly opened the door. "Babe, what's the matter?"

"Can I come in, please?" she asked softly.

He stood back and let her in. A million things were going through his mind as he tried to figure out why she was at his place so late. He wasn't going to lie, though; she looked damn good wearing a simple white summer dress and her hair in a messy bun. He wanted to strip that dress off of her and carry her upstairs so he could taste every inch of her.

"Rae, what's the matter? Is everything all right?" he asked with concern.

Lauryn took a deep breath. "I'm sorry for coming over so late, but I needed to apologize for the way I acted in your office the other day. I understand if you don't want to accept it."

She knew he was probably wondering why she couldn't just call or wait until the sun came up. After having the conversation with Jonathan, she knew she had to make things right with him.

He arched his eyebrows and folded his arms over his chest. He didn't say anything as he stared at her. A part of him was happy that she came over and admitted the error of her ways. The part that really worried him was why she came at 11PM to tell him when she could have called, sent a text, or emailed him. "Apology accepted, Beauty. I'm also sorry if I upset you in any way."

She smiled. Lauryn loved how he called her Beauty. "Okay, now that I apologized, I guess I can leave now."

Kenyon blocked her pathway." Oh, hell no, Lauryn. You're spending the night."

Lauryn tried to move past him, but he blocked her path. She knew that he was stronger than she was, but she wasn't spending the night with him.

"Excuse me, Kenyon."

Kenyon laughed because Lauryn was trying his faith. He looked down and zeroed in on her lips. In a spilt second, he pulled her close to his rock solid chest while moving his hand firmly to her hips. Lauryn wrapped her arms around his neck and, in that moment, his tongue entered her mouth. He swiftly pulled her closer and pinned her to the wall. When he heard her soft moans, it was music to his ears. His lips slowly moved down to her neck, kissing it softly and making small circles with his tongue.

Lauryn's body was on fire. She had never experienced anything like this in all of her twenty-four years of life. She felt she was being placed under a spell with each passing kiss. She knew if she didn't stop now, was going to be hard for her to break the spell that he had placed on her. She was going to enjoy the moment, though even for a short while.

She could feel her eyes rolling in the back of her head as he planted another kiss on her lips. "Kenyon, baby…." she said softly, feeling him move the strap of her dress down and kissing the tops of her breast. "Bedroom," she urged against his mouth.

He swooped her up into his arms and headed upstairs to his bedroom. He took two steps at a time and entered the room, placing her in the middle of the unmade king sized bed. He carefully removed her dress, followed by her bra. He stood in front of her, admiring her well-toned body, amazed at how beautiful she looked. He leaned in for a quick kiss on lips before looking into her eyes. He was prepared to see doubt or hesitation in them, but all he saw was pure passion.

He slowly stepped out of his pajama pants, which had Lauryn equally amazed. "Wow," she whispered. She was speechless to what she was seeing.

Kenyon gave her a sly smile. "You like what you see?" He asked with a hint of laughter.

She bounced her head similar to a bobble head. "I don't like what I see; I love what I see."

"Good to hear, Beauty," Kenyon whispered as he moved down to kiss and nibble on her thighs. He started to play with her clit, which was already swollen. He first started with a gentle stroke of his thumb. She jerked back, crying out in soft moans. He realized that she was enjoying it as he continued moving his thumb - gentle, soft, harder, faster, and slower

- until her whimpers turned to moans. Her nails dug deeper into his shoulder as her body shook with pure pleasure.

Lauryn watched him as he leaned over to grab a condom, tore it open with his teeth, and slowly placed it over his rock hard shaft. She gave a concerned look, wondering if it would fit; he wasn't a small man, and she sure as hell was a small woman.

She opened her leg to accept him freely. As soon as he entered her, she gasped, quickly feeling the effects of him inside of her. She hasn't had sex in almost two years, so she was definitely out of practice. She leaned into him as the pain subsided. She began to kiss his chest while moving her hips.

Kenyon couldn't believe the feeling he had once he entered Lauryn. He thought he had died and gone to heaven. For years he had imagined what it would be like to be with her intimately. They fit perfectly together; however, he was trying to take things slow when he saw the pained look on her face. It was evident that she hadn't had sex in a while; it was like she was a virgin once again. But as soon as she started moving her hips, Kenyon got down to business. He set the tempo by slowly thrusting in and out of her. He later picked up his speed, trying to make the moment last, as he felt his climax building.

"Baby, it feels like heaven," Lauryn moaned. Within moments, she was cumming and chanting his name over and over again.

"Beauty, I can't believe how good you feel. Can you please cum for me one more time? Just one more time for me, Rae?"

Her legs started shaking, and then she was cumming again while screaming his name. He couldn't take it any longer; he felt himself cumming, and the two climaxed together.

With that, Kenyon turned on his back with Lauryn still in his arms, never breaking their connection. Soon they were both in a deep slumber.

✳✳✳

Just before dawn, Lauryn felt Kenyon place kisses along her spine, getting her wet once again. She turned over and faced him. She didn't say anything as she placed her hand on his cheek. She pulled herself up and gave him a passionate kiss. Before Lauryn knew it, he was entering her once again; this time they made slow, passionate love, as if it was for the first time.

Lauryn woke up for the second time, only to be awakened by the morning sun. She turned and found that Kenyon was no longer in bed with her. She knew he probably had gone to practice. She got up and stretched, as part of her body was aching, but in a good way. She quickly went into the bathroom and looked at herself in the mirror. She noticed the passion marks that were placed on her body. She wasn't mad, but was more turned on by it.

"Damn you, Kenyon," she said to herself.

She was happy to find that he left a towel and toothbrush out. Lauryn was singing "Drunk in Love" by Beyonce at the top of her lungs as she stepped into the shower.

"So you're drunk in love?" Kenyon asked as he was behind her and started to caress her breasts.

She moaned. "I'm maybe drunk in love; who knows," she replied while turning around and kissing him.

"There is nothing better than morning kisses and a shower with my Beauty," Kenyon whispered. He pulled her closer as he kissed her neck. He leaned down, taking a nipple into his mouth. Lauryn arched her back and wrapped her legs around his waist, and with one quick move, Kenyon entered her.

"Will you spend the weekend with me?"

All Lauryn could say was, "Yes."

Chapter 9

It was midday when they came out of the shower, and the plan was for Lauryn to go home, get some clothes, and then they would go out to breakfast. That plan went out the window the second they made their way back into the bedroom. Kenyon really didn't know what happened, because Lauryn flipped the script on him. He was surprised when she went down on her knees and gave him the best blow job ever.

Kenyon looked over at her as she was sleeping so peacefully. Oh, how he wanted to wake her, but he knew she needed her rest. He slipped out of bed and headed downstairs to look for something to eat. He knew once Lauryn woke up, she was going to be like a baby bear. When looking through his freezer, he found shrimp, along with Lauryn's favorite: chicken wings. He learned that the night they were at The Stadium. He decided then to make grilled shrimp with fried wings and salad.

When Lauryn woke up, she noticed that Kenyon wasn't in bed again. She lay there for a few minutes before checking her phone. She was sure there were about a million texts from her parents, brothers, and friends. Sure enough, there were five missed calls from both of her parents, about six from her brothers, and a couple more from her friends, along with over 100 What's App messages. She quickly sent them a mass message letting them know that she was okay. She got up and went in to use the bathroom. When she came out, that was the first time she noticed her overnight bag by the door. She wondered when Kenyon had time to go and get it, or if Jonathan brought it over. At that point, she didn't care; all she wanted was some wings.

Kenyon was taking the last wing out of the deep fryer when he heard Lauryn walking down the stairs. He hoped she found her bag that he asked Jonathan to bring over for her, but most of all, he hoped she wasn't upset with him for calling her brother.

"I smell wings," she declared, walking past him and grabbing one. She stood there for a moment before grabbing another one. They were the best tasting wings she had in a long time! They were fried nice and light, and seasoned to the bone.

"I take it that you like the wings?" he asked, stealing a kiss.

"Yes, I do! They taste divine, babe. Just know you're going to have to make wings all the time now."

Kenyon laughed; Jonathan had told him the same thing when he stopped by. "Sure thing, baby, anything for you. Go and sit down at the table, and I'll bring your food."

Once Kenyon fixed their plates, they sat at the table and dug into their food. During their meal, the two talked about a variety of topics, including Kenyon's training and Lauryn's job at *The Bahamas Times*. Once they were done, they cleaned up the kitchen and headed into the family room. He turned on the radio as the soulful sounds of Mary J. Blige filled the room. Kenyon was going to use that time to get to know Lauryn, the woman whom he was falling in love with.

"Let's have a little chat."

"About?"

"I want to talk about you, Miss Lauryn Rae Smith."

She arched her eyebrow and pointed to herself. "Me?"

"Yes, you, baby." Kenyon interrupted with a smile.

"What do you want to talk about?" she continued.

"Whatever you want to tell me, sweetheart; tell me about your family."

Lauryn paused just before speaking. "Well, there is a saying that I am a part of 'Bahamian Royalty'."

"Mmm….Bahamian Royalty. Please do tell, Rae."

Lauryn shifted on the sofa to face Kenyon. "My family is called 'Bahamian Royalty' because both my maternal and paternal grandfathers have made history. My daddy's father's name was John Smith, and he was the youngest Chief Justice to be appointed. Then there is my mummy's daddy, Andrew Davis, who was the youngest Chief of Staff at Bahamas General Hospital. Then there are my parents; my daddy, is the youngest Commissioner of Police to hold that post. Then I have a bunch of aunties, uncles, and cousins who hold positions either in education, medicine, business, or tourism. Oh yeah, my granddaddies and dad were all appointed to their positions before their 50th birthdays." Lauryn left out her history moments, as she held a few records in the 100 and 200 meters at a couple of track meets.

Kenyon was impressed because her family members actually made history. "Wow, I understand why you say you're part of 'Bahamian Royalty'. So, are you and Jonathan the only children your parents have?"

"No, Johnny and I are the youngest; I have two older brothers, Ryan and Que, and a sister-in-law, Lena."

"I don't have to ask, but I'm sure you're a spoiled brat considering you're the only girl."

She smiled at him. Kenyon was caught off guard by her smile; he thought for sure she was going to put up a fuss. "Yes, I am a spoiled brat. With my older brother, Que, who is ten years older than I am, he has me so spoiled that he always says I am his baby. I used to sleep with him all the time growing up. Then there is my daddy, because I am his baby girl. What about you; do you spoil your baby sister?"

Kenyon laughed; anyone who knew him knew that Kennedy Makayla Jackson was the apple of his eye. "I would be lying to you, but yes, I do spoil my baby sister. Like I told you before, her name is Kennedy. With the eighteen year difference, people often believe that she is my child. Also, I play ref between her and my mommy because they look just alike, and they both have a smart mouth."

Lauryn laughed; she knew better than anyone that bumping heads with your mother could turn into full-fledged war. She and her mother, Angelica, bumped heads a lot, especially over the topic of Shannon. She felt the two were going to repeat history and become teenage parents like her and her husband, Max. Max and Angelica were fifteen and eighteen when they had their oldest son, Ryan.

It was hard at first because it was a long time before either one of their parents accepted they had a grandchild. Both Lauryn's grandparents were truly upset for their own selfish reasons. Her maternal grandparents were upset because her mother was only fifteen and in the 10th grade. Her paternal grandparents were upset because her father had a promising future as a lawyer. It was her great grandmother, Rae, who was the voice of reason, allowing Angelica and Max to move into her house.

While Angelica finished high school and Max joining the police force, they lived with Mama Rae until they got married three years later, and as a wedding present she gave them a piece of land. Once her mother graduated from high school, she went on to the University of the Bahamas, and then on to UWI. Her father worked his way up the ranks while going to school, also.

"I understand it's a mother/daughter thing around the world." She smiled.

"I know, that's the same thing my brother, Malik, says."

Kenyon nodded while flipping through his phone for a picture of his sister. He handed the phone over to her when he found one.

Lauryn looked at the picture and smiled. She understood why people felt she was his daughter; they look completely alike. She handed the phone back to him. "She's a pretty thing, but tell me about your bother."

"My brother, Malik, and I were born a month apart."

She arched her eyebrow. "A month apart, wow."

"My mommy had me when she was fifteen with a well-known drug dealer, Charles "Casino" Adderly..."

She put her hand up with a wide-eyed expression. "Hold up! Casino Adderly is your daddy?"

He nodded. "Yes, he is my father."

Lauryn was trying to find her words because she knew he was the biggest drug lord in the Bahamas. He was the father of the man she was in love with. "Wow, do you know if he's is in jail?" she asked softly.

Lisa got pregnant with Kenyon when she was fifteen, and Casino was five years her senior. She broke up with him not long after she had Kenyon because he refused to get out of the drug life. Kenyon knew his father all too well, despite not seeing him since he was six months old. His mother, Lisa, told him who his father was, and even showed pictures of him. She also had a picture of him holding Kenyon at the hospital when he was born.

He still remembered what his mother told him growing up, *"Do not fall in the footsteps of the man that made you, but the footsteps of the man that raised you."* Those words were etched in his mind and heart like a tattoo. "Yes, I know Casino is in jail, Rae. I know everything about him."

"Oh," she said, and continued looking at the pictures.

"As I was saying, my mommy hid me from Casino. After she had me, she went back to high school, and then to the University of the Bahamas to receive her degree in Primary Education. You remember when we were in the fourth grade and I left to go North Carolina?"

She nodded her head. "Yeah, I remember, Ken."

"Once we moved to North Carolina, my mummy basically put me in everything from track to football." He laughed, then continued speaking. "Malik was in the same boat as me, so we became best friends and started to hangout. Little did either one of us know, our parents were also hanging out with each other.

"While we were in our last year of middle school, they decided to get married, and we became one big happy family. During our last year of high school, Princess Kennedy Makayla Jackson joined the picture." Kenyon said happily.

Kenyon leaned his back on the sofa and didn't say anything for some time. He then looked at Lauryn, who looked as if she was deep in thought. Kenyon went into the kitchen and came back with a bowl of grapes.

"What's with the grapes?" she asked, taking a few for herself.

"I love grapes, and I'm not finish talking with you, either." He said with a huge smile.

"Fine, what else you want to talk about? I also love grapes, by the way," she said, taking a few more.

Kenyon debated on whether he should ask Lauryn about what happened between her and Shannon. He took a quick glance and saw something in her eyes which let him know that she wasn't ready to talk about it.

Chapter 10

Over the next month, Lauryn and Kenyon hung out ever chance they got. During that time they learned more about each other. He learned that she played the piano, was an awesome singer, and was fluent in Spanish. She was also a closet photographer. When he saw some of her photos, he was speechless. She definitely captured the essence of every picture she took. He saw a different side of her; not the stubborn side, but the more relaxed and funny side that wasn't afraid to enjoy life.

While he learned a lot about her, she learned that he also played the piano and the saxophone, and he was a remarkable singer. He also spoke fluently in French and Spanish, and had a love for race cars and motorcycles.

Kenyon looked at himself once more before heading out the door. Tonight they were going on their first official date to her favorite restaurant, Blue Anchor, followed by dancing at Calypso. After that, they would end the night with a nightcap at his place. They hadn't been together in almost a month, and the few times she had come over to his house, they'd had a heavy make-out session that left a few passion marks on her body. The reality was that Kenyon didn't want Lauryn to get the impression that they were in a relationship built purely on sex. The sex was off the charts; however, he wanted to be with her because he was in love with her. He wanted to be able to provide for her and give her the world.

Something they still hadn't addressed there where they stood, as well as what happened between her and Shannon, and why she no longer ran track. Something in his gut told him (he was going to get the full sense of what really went down in the upcoming weeks. He wasn't going to push her to talk about it, but he hoped she would tell him when the time was right.

Kenyon rang the doorbell, nervous as hell. Angelica opened the door and greeted him with a hug. "Good evening, Kenyon. How are you, sweetheart?"

Kenyon smiled. "I'm doing well, Mrs. Smith."

"Boy, what did I tell you about calling me Mrs. Smith?"

He sighed. She'd made it perfectly clear when he was over a few weeks ago to call her Gigi; that's what all her children's friends called her, and they called her husband Daddy Max. "I'm so sorry, I keep forgetting, Gigi."

She laughed softly. "That's okay. Come into the kitchen with me while I'm prepping Sunday dinner. Your woman doesn't know anything about the damn time."

Kenyon followed her into the kitchen and sat at the breakfast nook. "Don't worry, Gigi, Rae isn't late; our reservation isn't until 8 o'clock. I knew she was going be late. That's why I told her to be ready at 7."

"You're a smart man. You're learning about my child very fast."

She went on to ask him how training was going. She enjoyed hearing the happiness in his voice about getting ready for the World Games in Singapore, and the Olympics in Sidney. He then went on to ask if she was coming. Without any doubt, both her and her husband were going to be there. Not just to support him as her daughter's friend, but as her daughter's husband. A part of Angelica knew that Lauryn had found the one in Kenyon; a blind man could see that he was in love with her. More than anything, he was the factor in helping her child get back on the track.

Lauryn came down the stairs as she heard her mother and Kenyon laughing and talking. She knew that she was late; however, being on time wasn't her best quality. She got butterflies the second she entered the kitchen.

Kenyon stopped talking when he saw Lauryn enter the kitchen. She was wearing a royal blue fitted dress with a sweetheart neckline, and her hair was straightened from her usual kinky curls, which Kenyon loved.

"I know I'm late. I'm sorry, babes."

Getting up from the table, he gave her a soft kiss on her forehead, "That's okay, Beauty. You look pretty."

"Thanks, sweetheart."

Angelica stopped her task and smiled. "Y'all look like a power couple. Y'all had this planned with this royal blue and yellow?" she asked, noticing that they were matching.

They both stepped back and took a quick glance, noticing that they were, in fact, matching. Kenyon was wearing a royal blue jacket and yellow shirt that was open at the top with a pair of dark jeans. Lauryn looked down at her yellow pumps, and they started laughing. "Great minds think alike."

"I guess they do. Beauty, we really have to go if we don't want to be late."

"Okay, let me just grab my bag and we'll be on our way."

Angelica walked with them to the door. She didn't say anything when she saw Kenyon pick up Lauryn's overnight bag. She'd accepted a long time ago that her daughter was no longer a child. Besides, they'd had countless conversation about sex. More than anything, she was grateful that her children were never teenage parents.

"Enjoy yourself, guys, and be safe. Also, I expect you here for Sunday dinner," she said, kissing each of them on their cheeks.

"We will, mommy. And yes, we will be here for dinner."

"Enjoy your night, Gigi."

It was ten to eight when they pulled into the front of Blue Anchor. The valet opened the door for Kenyon and he handed the young man his key before coming around to open Lauryn's door. One thing his step-father taught him was that a man always opened the door for a lady.

"Watch your step," he said as they walked into the restaurant.

Lauryn knew all eyes were on them from the second they stepped into the restaurant. She wasn't mad; she knew she was a show-stopper. What Lauryn enjoyed the most about having Kenyon on her arm was that he gave her a sense of calmness that she never experienced in her life. However, a part of her knew not to let her guard down too much; Lauryn knew she couldn't bear another heartbreak.

She hadn't see Shannon since that day during her lunch break. Lauryn didn't like that, either, because when Shannon was quiet, that only meant he was up to something. She needed to tell Kenyon, along with her family, about the abuse she dealt with from him. She knew she couldn't start a relationship with Kenyon without being honest.

The hostess showed them to their table, and they were seated on the outside deck overlooking Nassau Harbor. It was a very picturesque night, as two cruise ships were on the dock, and the old lighthouse was shining brightly in the distance from the Sir Sidney Poitier Bridge. Once the hostess got their drink orders, she left the two as they looked over the menu. Blue Anchor was known for their various seafood dishes, so Kenyon already knew what he wanted. Lauryn, however, was undecided.

Kenyon placed the menu down and stared at her. It seemed as if she got even more beautiful every time he saw her. He loved her hair straight, but he liked it more when it was kinky and curly. Then again, it didn't matter to him because she was beautiful, regardless.

He found it damn cute right now, and because of her facial expression, it told him that she was unsure about what she wanted.

Kenyon placed his hand over hers, "Don't worry, Rae, I'll make you some wings tomorrow." He said with a slight chuckle.

Lauryn started laughing because he'd read her mind perfectly. Most times she went out, the first thing she looked for on the menu was wings. "I'll hold you to that, Kenyon."

By the time the hostess returned, she had made up her mind about her order. Kenyon ordered the grilled salmon, while Lauryn ordered the steak and lobster.

Kenyon took a sip of his drink as a million things went running through his mind. He still wanted to know what happened between her and Shannon. It still annoyed him that she shared her body with him, but not her past. He knew his grandmother always said, *"Let sleeping dogs lie…"* This was one dog he wasn't willing to let lie. He knew he needed to be smart about the way he handled things; he didn't want to push her away, especially with how far they'd come in such a short period of time. More than anything, he didn't want to upset her in any way. He knew it was kind of too late to ask, because they'd already had sex, but he wanted her to be his girlfriend.

Lauryn could tell that he was deep in thought about something. Her gut was telling her it had something to do with her past. Oh, how she wanted to tell Kenyon about her relationship with Shannon. A part of her was still afraid; she had only been totally honest with Mia and Renée about what happened. She wasn't going to allow Satan's first born, Shannon, to mess up her time with Kenyon, but she needed to know what was going between them.

"Lauryn, I want to ask you a question."

"Okay, what do you want to ask?"

He took a deep breath. "I want to know if you want to be my girlfriend."

Lauryn didn't say anything. She looked at him and smiled. No guy had ever asked her to be their girlfriend. He made her feel special, almost like a queen.

"Why should I be your girlfriend?" she asked playfully.

"You should be my girlfriend because you're my Beauty. To me, that means you're prefect for me."

"I'll be honored to be your girlfriend, Kenyon. I ask that you respect me and, most of all, always support me."

Kenyon smiled. "That's easy like Sunday morning."

He leaned in to give her a kiss to seal their commitment to one another. When they heard someone clear their throat, they looked up to see Shannon and Lauryn's friend, Shay.

"Lauryn, you never kissed me like that," Shannon said. He stared at Lauryn without even acknowledging Kenyon.

Lauryn sucked her teeth because she really wasn't in the mood for Shannon and his bullshit. More than anything, she was shocked that Shay was with Shannon. She couldn't be mad at her, though, because she never really talked about her relationship with anyone outside of Mia and Renée. "Hello Shannon. Shay."

Kenyon didn't say anything; right now, the only thing on his mind was to get up and slap the piss out of Shannon, but he was taking his cue from Lauryn and how she was being a real lady.

"You're not going to answer my damn question?" He said loudly. At that point, he was getting annoyed as hell with her. He really didn't care that they were in a public place, or the fact that Shay, the bitch, was on his arm.

Lauryn looked around and noticed people were staring. She was getting embarrassed and wanted to leave before someone noticed her. Next thing she knew, they would probably be all over social media.

"No, she not is going to answer your question. I ask that you speak to my girlfriend in a better tone," Kenyon demanded.

Shannon was laughing his head off. He knew, for sure, that Kenyon had lost his damn mind saying that Lauryn was his girlfriend. He didn't care what anyone said; she would always be his, even if that meant beating her ass until she got the message.

"You're really funny. Don't let this bitch on my arm fool you. Lauryn will always be my woman."

Lauryn placed her hand over her mouth. She was shocked that Shay was standing there letting Shannon disrespect her. At that point, Lauryn knew she had heard enough. "Enough! Kenyon, can we please go?"

Kenyon got the attention of their host.

Shay started laughing because, in true Lauryn fashion, she was running away. "Like always, your ass is running away."

Lauryn looked at her and laughed. "Shay, karma is a bitch, and she's going to rock your damn world."

She looked back over at Shannon, and everything he did came flashing right before her eyes.

"Be careful. Mark my words."

✳✳✳

Kenyon made it to his apartment in record time. He could tell that Lauryn was hurt, but he wasn't going to allow Shannon and Shay to jack up their first date. He came around to help her out of the truck, knowing, for sure, she needed to relax first. Once they were inside, he swept her up in his arms and headed straight for his bedroom. He placed her on the bed while he went to run some water for her.

Lauryn hadn't said anything since they left the restaurant. She was too embarrassed and hurt to even speak. She was embarrassed by Shannon's actions, and hurt to see Shay on his arm all happy and shit like the Kool-Aid Man. For years, Renée said Shay wanted to be her, but she thought Renée was just hating on her; her actions were proven to be correct tonight. Lauryn just hoped she was careful; Shannon wasn't an easy man to love.

"I'm so sorry, Kenyon," she said softly.

Kenyon put his hand up. "Listen to me, Lauryn Rae Smith, never apologize for someone else's actions, especially a jackass like Shannon. Understand?"

"Yes, I understand."

"Good, sweetie," he said, giving her a soft kiss on her lips. "Come and relax in the tub for a while, and then we'll can find something to eat."

Lauryn looked up at Kenyon. She knew she was falling in love with him, but a part of her wasn't ready to do just that. She knew she needed to deal with her past first before she told him how she really felt.

He placed her in the tub. "I'll be back, just relax."

Kenyon came back into the bathroom, only to find Lauryn asleep. He stood there and watched her for a second, looking like a black sleeping beauty. He woke her up with soft kisses all over her face, making her slowly give him a beautiful smile. "I guess I fell asleep."

"Yes, you did," Kenyon replied. He grabbed a towel, dried her off, and placed his college track shirt on her.

When Lauryn entered the bedroom, she was speechless. Candles were lit everywhere, and a blanket was placed on the floor. The sound of Sam Smith's soulful voice was playing in the background as she slowly looked around.

"This isn't what I had planned for our first date," Kenyon admitted.

"It's okay, sweetheart. I love it."

They made their way onto the blanket, where a bowl of strawberries, some whipped cream, and a bottle of white wine were set. They spent the rest of the night talking about their lives. Kenyon told her about his line brothers and some of the madness they had experienced while they were in college. Lauryn was excited to meet them after he informed her they were coming to visit at some point during the summer. She went on to talk about her upcoming plans for the articles she was working on, including the Golden Knights and the Golden Girls. They also talked a little more about what they wanted out of their relationship. It was shortly after three when they fell asleep in each other's arms.

Chapter 11

It was three days before Kenyon's grandparents' party, and Lauryn was in her favorite store with Renée and Mia looking for an outfit. Lauryn emerged from the dressing room for the sixth time that afternoon. "So, what do you think?" she asked, turning around in full circle for both of them to see.

"I like this one better than the first five you tried on," Mia said, coming up next to her.

Renée frowned and replied, "I am not a fan of this; besides, you have like a million and one outfits in your closet to wear."

"I know, Ren, but I just want to look nice for Champ's grandparent's party, that's all," she said, then headed back into the dressing room.

"It sounds serious; you're attending family functions after two weeks of dating," Mia said.

Lauryn shouted, "Mia, it's not that deep! Besides, like I told you, I met both of his grandparents. I don't see what the big deal is."

"I agree with both of you," Renée said, pointing to Mia. "I agree with you because it must be a serious relationship if he's taking Rae as his date." Then she pointed to Lauryn, who headed over to the rack, looking for something else to wear. "And I totally agree with Rae that it's not that deep."

The three women started to laugh because Renée always agreed with everyone when they knew it didn't matter to her. Lauryn grabbed another dress - this one black lace- from the rack. When she emerged from the dressing room, both Mia and Renée were speechless. "So, what do you think?"

"Yes, that's definitely the one, Rae," Renée said.

"Lucky for you, black happens to be your favorite color," Mia said.

"Yes, black is your color, Mia Gayle," Lauryn said, heading back into the dressing room.

"Gal, you did not tell me Champ had a daughter," Mia said.

"Champ doesn't have a daughter!" Lauryn shouted from the dressing room. She came out and saw Tayshaun, Jonathan, Kenyon, a little girl who she knew to be Kennedy, and also his brother, Malik, coming into the store. Tayshaun leaned in and brushed a kiss on Renée's lips, while Kenyon did the same to Lauryn.

"Baby, I want you to meet my brother, Malik, and my baby sister, the infamous Kennedy." Malik leaned in and give her a kiss on the cheek. Lauryn studied his face. He and Kenyon might not be related by blood, but they were related by looks and sexiness. He stood at about six-five and was a bit darker then Kenyon. His hair was cut close to his scalp, and his eyes were jet black. He was also fit, as his outfit consisted of a red fitted tee and khaki shorts that showed off his body.

"It's nice to meet you, Lauryn," Malik said with a thick Southern accent.

She smiled and got to eye level with the prettiest little girl she had ever seen. "Hey, pretty girl, I'm Lauryn, the one you talked to the other night on the phone," she happily said.

"I'm Kennedy, and you sound different on the phone. Are you Champ's girlfriend? Because he never answered me when I asked on the phone," she asked boldly.

Lauryn looked up at Kenyon, wide-eyed, and started to laugh. "You could say that."

Kenyon just shook his head and introduced Malik and Kennedy to Mia and Renée. He was totally embarrassed; Kennedy didn't pull any punches when she started asking questions. She grilled Mia, wanting to know why she didn't have a boyfriend like Renée and Lauryn. She also asked her brother, Malik, if he wanted to be Mia's boyfriend. Malik quickly ended her round of questioning with an annoyed expression.

"Did you find something to wear, baby?" Kenyon asked Lauryn, who was headed to the register.

"Yes, I did. I'm going classic with black and red," she said happily.

Kenyon stopped and looked at the woman who had been on his mind for the last two weeks. He couldn't wait until the party to see her dress, and also show her off to his family. He knew, for sure, his grandmother and sister liked Lauryn, so that was good a sign.

Lauryn was about to hand the cashier the money when Kenyon pushed her hand aside and paid for the dress. "I could pay for my own dress, Kenyon," she snapped.

He looked down at her and knew she was upset. Another thing he'd learned about her was that she was very independent. "I know you can, baby," he said as he brushed a soft kiss across her temple. He took the bag from the cashier and smiled.

When they left the store, the gang decided to go for lunch at Pink Sand, a local restaurant on Paradise Island near the famous Bahama Resorts. They all had a good time laughing, mostly because little Kennedy was entertaining everyone with her never-ending questions.

Shannon was sitting at the far end of the restaurant when he noticed Lauryn walking in. He was super annoyed when he saw Kenyon kiss her. He had to break up this little relationship that was going on between them, and fast.

He kept a close eye on her when she got up from her bar stool and moved away from the table. He slowly got up from his bar stool, walked to the back of the restaurant, and waited for her to come out of the restroom.

As Lauryn came out, she jumped when she saw Shannon standing by the door. "Oh, fuck!"

"Your mouth is dirty."

Lauryn tried to move past him, but he blocked her. "Shannon, please move."

He didn't budge, so Lauryn slapped him. He was shocked by her actions. Lauryn quickly walked past him, scared that he would retaliate, but he wouldn't. One thing she knew about Shannon was that he wasn't going to try anything with her brothers, or Tayshaun, nearby.

She hurried back to the table, looking over her shoulder to see if he followed her. She took a deep breath to calm her nerves.

Jonathan looked at his sister, sensing something was wrong. He didn't want to cause a big scene, so he'd wait until later to ask.

He looked around and saw Shannon leaving from the same direction Lauryn just came from. He didn't mention anything, but he knew she needed deal to with Shannon once and for all.

Chapter 12

"Baby, you look fine," Kenyon complimented when he glanced at Lauryn. When he got to her house to pick her up, he was speechless. She was wearing a black lace strapless cocktail dress with a red bow in the middle, and the sexiest pair of red heels he had ever seen. Her hair was pulled up in ponytail like a ballerina. She completed the outfit with light makeup and a pair of diamond stud earrings.

"You sure, Kenyon?" she asked as she looked at him. He was wearing a black pair of dress pants, a red dress shirt, which was unbuttoned, and a black blazer with two diamond studs in each ear. Lauryn gave a wide smile at the man who had been taking over her heart for the last few weeks. She often found herself smiling in the middle of the day because she either was thinking about him, or Kenyon would text, *"I miss you, baby,"* or *"Enjoy your day, lady…"* or just something sweet. The sex was even better; Lauryn found herself sometimes just showing up to his house in nothing but a sundress and no panties. However, this weekend they both were on dry dock because his parents and siblings were staying with them.

He pulled his truck in the spot behind his cousin CJ's car. Kenyon came around and helped her out, leaning down to give her a passionate kiss. He moved his hands around her waist as she wrapped her arms around his neck.

He knew he could never get tired of kissing her. Even when they ninety and ninety-one, he would still want to kiss her. Kenyon was definitely putting his tongue skills to use as he moved it around every inch of her mouth.

She was glad that he was holding her, because she was getting weak at the knees as he continued to kiss her. Every emotion was running through her body like ToNique Williams-Darling in Athens. Kenyon was taking everything out of her, right down to the gum she was chewing.

They continued kissing for another five minutes before Kenyon decided to release her mouth. He knew for a fact that if he didn't, things would have gone a bit further. They just looked at each other and smiled. Lauryn moved her arms from around his neck and wiped away all the evidence of their kiss.

She chuckled and spoke at the same time. "You're wearing red lipstick, Kenyon."

"I've been told red is my color," he said with a wide smile.

"That may be true. But I don't think it's your color when it comes to your lips."

"So what is the color when it comes to my lips?" he smugly asked.

She didn't hesitate when she answered his question. "You're a natural pink, Champ."

"Natural color, I see. I think the best color for me is pink, too. Like my good friend, Piglet."

Lauryn laughed; Kenyon always had something smart to say. Just in that moment she licked her lips and realized they were slightly swollen. She didn't want the first time meeting his mother to be a disaster because her lips were swollen.

"Damn!" she muttered under her breath.

"On the subject of lips, I hate to tell you, Rae, but they are slightly swollen," he said softly.

"I know, Kissing Bandit," she said as she put on more lipstick.

"Kissing Bandit. I kind of like that, baby," he said, and leaned in to brush a soft kiss on her lips.

Lauryn smiled. She couldn't believe how hard and fast she was falling for him. Well, she always had a little crush on him. Now that little crush from primary school was full blown to love. It was scary for I think this should be her because she made a promise eighteen months ago that she would never fall in love with anyone. Now she was doing just that with Kenyon.

"You ready, Rae?" he asked, gently grabbing her hand.

"Yes, I am, Champ," she said happily.

Kenyon and Lauryn heard the music coming from the backyard as they walked along the path that lead to the party. "Wow," was all Lauryn could whisper when she saw how nicely decorated the yard was with the colors red and black. As the waiter passed her, she grabbed a glass of champagne for the both of them.

Lauryn took a long sip because she was nervous as hell. "Come on, baby, let me introduce you to my mommy and aunties." Kenyon guided her to the table where his mother and aunties were sitting. Lauryn didn't have to ask which one was his mother; her eyes were just like Kenyon's.

"Good evening!" they all said in unison. Kenyon pulled Lauryn close by his side.

Lauryn saw eight pairs of eyes glaring at her. She simply smiled. She knew they were sizing her up, and fast, at that. Kenyon introduced her to his three aunties, Bridgette, Karen, and Yvette first, then to his mother, Lisa, who, at the age of thirty-eight, did not look a day over thirty.

"Lisa, I would like for you to meet my girlfriend, Lauryn."

Lauryn extended her hand for a handshake, but Lisa got up from the table and gave Lauryn a big hug. "Nice to finally meet you, sweetheart. Kenyon has told me so much about you."

She ushered Lauryn to an empty seat next to her and asked for her to sit down. "Champ, go and get Lauryn and me something to drink, she ordered her son. He didn't bother to ask either one of them what they wanted; knew what they liked to drink. He walked off to the bar and said a quick prayer because he knew his mother and his aunties would get really personal with their Q&A.

Kenyon saw his six cousins - Justin, CJ, Hakeem, Christian, Myron and Kyle - along with his brother, Malik, standing by the bar. "Damn, Champ, you left your girl with my mummy and Lisa, Sonya, and Karen," Justin said in surprise.

"Can I have two white wines and one Gin and tonic with water?" he told the bartender before responding to his cousin, Justin, who knew how intimidating his mother and aunties could be. "I'm not worried; Lauryn can handle herself."

"I hope so. I love my mother dearly, but shit, Sonya can take it to the next level," Hakeem said.

Everyone nodded in agreement. They each knew how their mothers operated.

"So, Champ, you only been home a couple of weeks already, and you find yourself a girlfriend. Damn, you don't waste any time," C.J said.

Kenyon waited a minute to answer because he hadn't taken his eyes off of the table where his mother and aunties was sitting. Now, it looked like his three female cousins, T'Vonya, Crystal, and April, had joined the table. He didn't mind because it looked as if Lauryn was holding her own with everyone, especially his cousin Crystal, who was known to be little rude at times.

"What can I say, I get what I want. Besides, Lauryn and I go way back to St. Dominic."

"Just like that, Champ!" his cousin Kyle said.

The cousins smiled and laughed because they knew how much of a smart ass Kyle was, and how much they looked up to their older cousin. Especially because the Carter cousins were known for their damn good looks, ability to get what they wanted, and, most of all, have women going off the deep end for them. Kenyon didn't have to live in Nassau to know that everyone knew his cousins, mainly the ladies. CJ and Justin made the blueprint for their younger cousin when it came to women. They each followed it, and made a few adjustments along the way.

Kenyon decided to talk with his cousins, because Lauryn's facial expression told him she was good, even though he would love to be a fly on the wall to hear what questions they were asking her. He knew for a fact that his grandmother already told them who her family was, but they were asking to sate their curious minds.

***

"You're so small for twenty-four especially since I know that Max is your daddy," Kenyon's aunt Karen said.

Lauryn smiled and prayed they did not know her face from track, and for being plastered all over the island for her athletic skills. To her surprise, the Carter women didn't intimidate her like she was expecting. They actually were sweet people who asked a lot of questions, but she wasn't bothered by that one bit. She was already prepared for them because of the Q&A Kenyon's little sister gave her not too long ago. She could tell that they may be sweet, but if you crossed any one of these women, and it would be hell to pay.

Each sister's personality was not hard to figure out: The oldest, Bridgette, was an RN and, naturally, the mother hen among the sisters who tried to keep the peace. Yvette was the second oldest and an Assistant General Manager at Bahamas Resorts. She was the quiet storm of the bunch, but God help you if you crossed her. There was Karen, who was the third oldest. She was an HR Manager for the Ministry of Tourism, and she had a larger than life personality. Lisa was the youngest, and was a Special Education teacher in North Carolina. She could hold her own among her sisters. Lauryn knew about that, because the women in her family were no different.

They asked about her family, her job, and school first before asking about her relationship with Kenyon. She told them the honest truth about their relationship, which was still pretty new. Of course the topic of Kenyon coming home to train for the World Games came up. Lauryn frowned inwardly because she knew it wouldn't be long before his aunties realized who in the hell she was.

"Lauryn, have you been to any of Champ's practices yet?" his mother asked.

"No, ma'am, I haven't. Most of the time, when he's at practice, I'm at work. For the last couple of Saturdays, I have been working on a special piece," she said truthfully.

"I understand. I know you'll be out there tomorrow afternoon at his track meet, for sure, I'm going along with his dad, his brother, and sister. Actually, everyone plans to go to support him," she said with a smile.

Lauryn forced a smile. She and Kenyon had already had a conversation about the track meet that the BAA was holding tomorrow for the people who were training for the World Games and the Olympic. As much as she didn't want to, she had to cover the story for the paper.

"I will be there. I'm working tomorrow from the press box."

"That's right! You work for the newspaper as a sports writer."

"Yes, ma'am, I work for *The Bahamas Times*."

They talked for a while before Kenyon finally came with their drinks, along with his cousins and his brother. His cousins, Kyle and Myron, knew who she was right off the bat. She had graduated a year before them. Those two were always trying to get rich quick. They would sell each other if it were possible.

. "Champ, you didn't tell us that Rae was your girl," Myron said with a huge smile. They both leaned in and give her a peck on her cheek.

"Baby, you know these two fools?" Kenyon asked, pulling Lauryn closer to him. Kenyon knew his cousin really had to know who she was, because they called her by her middle name.

"Yes, I know Kyle and Myron. They went to East with me, and graduated a year after me." Lauryn went to East Providence High School; it's one of the top ranked schools in the Bahamas in both athletics and academics.

"Oh."

Myron tapped his mother, Karen, and said, "Mummy, do you know who Rae is? You should remember. I think it was in '09 at

The Caribbean Junior Games. We kept saying how small she was to be so fast."

From the second Caribbean left his mouth, Lauryn wanted to crawl under a rock and die. She knew it was not going to be long before someone realized who she was. Those games were special to her because they were her last, and she also set a few records along the way.

"Oh, damn, it is Goldie, Myron," she said, not taking her eyes off Lauryn. Goldie was the name that Keith Michaels, a well-known sports reporter from St. Kitties had given her; that was because, during her first Caribbean Games, she won five gold medals.

"Lauryn, sweetheart, you used to run track?" Lisa asked.

She took a deep breath and forced a smile. "Yes, but I hung my sprints up about year and a half ago."

"Why?" Karen asked in an inquisitive voice.

She looked around at everyone before staring at Kenyon. "I got injured, so I decided to hang them up." Lauryn got injured, all right, but it wasn't any of her bones; just an injured soul and confidence.

Kenyon knew she was uncomfortable when she went stiff in his arms. He quickly changed the subject before everyone started asking her more questions. "Yes, Rae is Goldie, and I think you ladies have asked her more than enough questions for the night. It's time I take my baby onto the dance floor. Kenyon led her over to the dance floor, where quite a number of people were dancing. Even his grandparents were dancing.

A slow song began to play as they started to dance. He could tell that everyone was watching them.

"Thanks," she said softly.

"Don't worry about it, but baby, you're going to have to tell me what the real reason is for hanging up you sprints," he said.

"I know, but I'm not ready yet, Champ. It still hurts," she said with heartache.

"I know it still hurts, baby. When you're ready, I'll be ready to listen," he said as he brushed a kiss on her forehead.

They danced to four more songs together. Before they knew it, each one of his cousins, and his brother, wanted a dance with her. Lauryn had a blast dancing with each of his cousins because she learned something new about Kenyon. Myron and Kyle had her laughing the most, and they were the only two who could keep up with her on the dance floor.   His three female cousins, April, Crystal, and T'Vonya, invited her to their next girls' night. She also shared a dance with his grandfather. She realized then how Kenyon would look at his age. Lauryn thought how lucky she would be to become Mrs. Kenyon Carter. She would hit the jackpot because Robert Carter was one nice looking man, and also a sweet soul, and Kenyon looked so much like him. She was in love with him.

***

It was close to four o'clock when Kenyon bought her home. Kenyon told her to call in sick if she wasn't ready to face the track. Lauryn knew, deep down, she couldn't do that to herself, especially if it affected her job, or meant not supporting Kenyon. Yet she was still frustrated because she was still allowing the pain and anger to take over her life. For the first time in her life, she questioned her loyalty to herself, and to the person that she loved.

Chapter 13

Lauryn lay awake in her bed, crying, because she didn't know what to do. Her loyalty had always been a key to her personality. Now, more than ever, she felt she was not being loyal to the man that she loved so deeply. She continued to lay there and get her thoughts together about going to the track. Lauryn knew for a fact that Shannon was going to be present, and she would have to interview him.

She sighed. "I love him…" she said to herself. Lauryn realized she couldn't allow Shannon to cause her to be a prisoner in her own life. At some point she would have to wake up and smell the coffee with him, and move on with her life. She was going to start today.

She picked up the phone and called Mia. After the third ring, she picked up, and it was obvious that she was still half-asleep.

"Mia Gayle, what are you doing today?" she asked.

"What I'm doing now, sleeping, so call me back in a few hours," Mia said sleepily.

"Be ready at three. You're going to work with me today."

Mia had already started to fall back to sleep. "Okay, I got you, Rae."

Before Lauryn knew it, the line went dead. She shook her head. One thing about Mia was that she slept like a newborn baby. Lauryn laid back down to catch a few more hours of sleep; she had danced until 3 AM.

***

Kenyon picked up the phone to call Lauryn a few times, but changed his mind. He knew she was going to be at the track, but, deep down, he knew if she had a choice, she wouldn't be covering the meet.

Kenyon took a deep breath and rubbed his hand over this face in frustration. He just wanted to pop Shannon's neck for what he did to her.

He glanced at his phone and, to his surprise, it was already midday. He went downstairs to see his mother in the kitchen sipping on a glass of juice and reading on her laptop. "Good morning, Lisa, or should I say good afternoon," he said while walking over to the fridge to pour a glass of juice and make a bowl of cereal.

She looked over her glass and smiled. "Yes, good afternoon."

They sat in a comfortable silence for a few minutes. Kenyon's mind went straight to Lauryn as he thought about how beautiful she looked last night, and how well she got along with the women in his family. She fit right in with the family, which, for him, was wonderful.

"Champ, Lauryn is a pretty girl, but I felt as if she was holding back when Karen started asking her why she stopped running."

Kenyon was not surprised at his mother's statement. Just like his grandmother, she had a sixth sense when it came to people and their true feelings.

Kenyon sighed. "Yes, she is holding something back. I'm not pushing her to talk about it, either, but it has something do with her ex-boyfriend. I don't know what he did to her, but whatever it was really hurt her. I trust and love Rae, and when the time is right, she's going to tell me what happened," he said, taking a deep breath.

Lisa just looked at her oldest child. She didn't just think of him as her child, but as one of her best friends. He was the spitting image of her father. She continued to stare at him, seeing a man who was in love, but was also frustrated because he could not help the one he loved.

Her mind went back on his father, Casino, because she could remember when his sister, Kenya, was in the similar situation with her ex-boyfriend, Michael, who physically abused her and didn't want her to be with anyone else. Casino was unsure about what was going on with Kenya, and the day he finally decided to ask about what was going on was the day that she was killed by her boyfriend. Even though Lisa had not seen Casino in more than twenty years, she could see the same facial expression on her son's face, and it was killing her.

"Champ, I know you don't want to push the issue with Rae and her ex, but baby, you may have to; the frustrated look on your face is the same one your father had when his sister, Kenya, was in the same boat. Do you know who you were named after?"

He shook his head.

"You were named after Casino's sister, and my best friend, Kenya Erica. She was killed by her boyfriend the day before you were born, which was Kenya's 16th birthday. Just like you, he trusted and loved Kenya enough that she would tell him what was going on with her and Michael."

Lisa sighed before she continued. "I still could remember when Dunce, your dad's best friend, called to give him the news about Kenya. That was the first time I've ever seen your father cry. When he found out that Michael was the one who killed her, he was distraught. That was the day he had finally decided to ask Kenya about her relationship with Michael. Unfortunately, his suspicions were true, and he felt he didn't do anything about it."

Lisa started crying because she saw the same frustration in Kenyon as she saw in Casino twenty-five years earlier.

Lisa and Kenya had been best friends since they were eleven years old. They were the total opposite in every sense. Kenya was more laid back, down-to-earth, smart, and the quiet one, while Lisa was the outgoing drama queen who was daring, smart, and the life of the party. They did have one thing in common, though; they wanted to grow up fast. Both had the opportunity to, and they both paid a heavy price for it. Kenya lost her life while Lisa got pregnant.

He leaned in and gave his mother a kiss. "Thanks for telling me that happened. I will most definitely ask Rae about hers and Shannon's relationship. I have to go before Jimmy starts calling. Love you," Kenyon said and kissed his mother again.

Lisa smiled at Kenyon. "I love you too, baby."

She sat there, watching her child walk out of the kitchen, and smiled. Kenyon might have looked like her father, but he was most definitely Casino's child.

Chapter 14

Mia looked over at her best friend, completely nervous about going to the track.

"Are you ready, Lauryn?" Mia asked, giving Lauryn a concerned look.

Lauryn smiled. "I am more than ready."

Mia gave her a wicked smile. "Well, in that case, one more make-up check and let's go cheer on your man."

Lauryn rolled her eyes and laughed at Mia's statement. Yes, Kenyon was her man, there was no question about it.

Lauryn walked into the stadium for the first time in eighteen months. She felt a thousand different emotions all at once. The last time Lauryn stepped foot in this stadium was to tell Jimmy that she was no longer running track. She would never forget that day, because the conversation was still fresh in her mind…

"Rae, what do you mean you no longer want to run track? Are you pregnant? What is it, my baby girl? Just tell me why you no longer want to run," he asked all in one breath.

Lauryn still couldn't remember seeing anything put pure pain in his eyes, and hearing fear in his voice. She looked at the man who was a second father to her and told him a bold face lie. "No, I'm not pregnant. I just don't have the love for the sport the way I used to anymore. Besides, I can't handle the pressure of being a reporter and athlete at the same time. I'm really home sick," she said softly.

Jimmy just looked at her because he knew she was lying. One thing he knew about Rae was that she could handle whatever came her way. That's what made her so special. If his gut was right, he knew that damn boy, Shannon Knowles, who Rae was in love with, had something to do with it.

He took a deep breath and arched his eyebrow. "Rae, are you sure this is what you want, baby girl?"

Lauryn nodded. "Yes, sir. Thank you."

Jimmy smiled. "Baby girl, whenever you are ready to rebuild on your legacy, I'm to here help you. I love you."

She walked out his office and started to cry, because lying to Jimmy, of all people, was a sin within a sin...

"Lauryn! Lauryn! Lauryn!" Mia said, waving her hands in front of her face.

"Yeah, Mia, sorry I was somewhere else," she said.

Mia studied her face. "Are you sure you're up for this?"

"Of course I am, Mia. I'm here to do my job, and also support my man," she said with a smile.

"There goes Malik," Mia said, and they walked over to him.

They lean in and hugged him. "Hey ladies, how are you doing?" he said, never taking his eyes off of Mia.

"I am doing just fine, Malik. How are you doing?" Mia asked with a smile.

"Have a slight hangover, but other than that, I'm doing fine."

Lauryn arched her eyebrow and smiled. Malik was feeling Mia, just like she was feeling Malik. .

"Mia Gayle, are you going to sit in the press box with me o-,"

Mia interrupted her without taking her eyes off Malik "No, I think am going to sit with Malik."

"Okay, I will see you later." Lauryn watched Mia and Malik head to their seats. She shook her head and moved toward the press box.

Kenyon kept looking in the press box, hoping he would see Lauryn. He continued to look until he saw her coming towards him. She was wearing his favorite color: a red *Bahamas Times* polo shirt and khaki slacks. Her hair was pulled back in a ponytail, and she completed the outfit with a pair of diamond studs.

She gave him a million dollar smile before speaking. "Hey, Kenyon, do you mind if I ask you a few question?"

"No, you can ask me anything you want, sweetheart," he said smoothly.

Lauryn set up her tape recorder. She knew for a fact that Kenyon was watching her, and she could feel the passion.

"Okay, I'm ready. I'm only going to ask you few questions," she said, and clicked record on the machine.

Lauryn's interview with Kenyon only lasted for five minutes. She quickly ran through the questions, because her mind was telling her to stop the recording and kiss him. After she was done with Kenyon, she interviewed the Sands Twins, Ahmad and Rashad. Lauryn also enjoyed interviewing the twins because of their outgoing personality. That, and they were in love with her. She then interviewed her teammates from the 2007, 2008, and 2009 National Caribbean Junior Games: Alyssa Johnson, Simone Robert, and Brittany Archer. They made up the under 17 and under 20 4x1 relay team, and had won gold. Then there were Vincent Thompson, Antonia Clark-Lewis, Chandra Knowles-Williams, and Keith Brown, who also won gold medals in previous Olympic Games. She was able to interview the Golden Knight, Chris Brown, too.

Lauryn was happy to see Sammy Munroe, and she knew Kenyon was even happier, since he had always been his idol. Even though Lauryn was working, she felt right at home. She realized then how much she missed the track.

***

Shannon watched Lauryn most of the day as she interviewed everyone except him. He also watched her flirting with Kenyon every chance she got. Shannon noticed, for the first time, she was by herself. He walked up behind her and tapped her shoulder. Lauryn jumped and dropped her cell phone.

She sighed and started cursing under her breath. "What the hell is your problem, Shannon?" she asked with annoyance, picking up her cell phone. He laughed and gave her a sly smile.

"My problem is you, Lauryn. All day I have been watching you interview everybody out here, and then watched you totally disrespect me by flirting with your boy, Kenyon," he said, running his hand over her forearm.

Lauryn moved back and arched her eyebrows. "Shannon, let me tell you something about disrespect. Your ass disrespected me every time you put your hands on me, or when you talked down to me, or when you tried to force yourself on me. That's disrespect."

He didn't say anything as Lauryn glanced at him. She saw the look in his eyes, which she knew all too well.

He squeezed her arm so tight she knew for a fact that it would bruise. "Be careful what you say to me, bitch, about me disrespecting you, because that can always be arranged," Shannon said, and released her arm.

Lauryn looked at him and rubbed her arm. "If I were you, I would be careful what I say. I can always arrange for your ass to be arrested for making threats on my life."

Shannon pushed her against the gate and squeezed her face. "I don't make threats, but I do make promises, bitch," he fumed. He leaned against her, kissing her lips before walking away.

Lauryn put her hand over her face and started to cry. She felt so dirty because Shannon had kissed and touched her.

"I need to get the hell out of here," she whispered.

Just as she walked off to find Mia, she ran into Jimmy. He looked at the woman who was like his daughter. He pulled her into a tight hug and didn't say anything. Lauryn felt safe in Jimmy's arms because, no matter what happened, he would always be her sergeant father.

"Baby girl, it's so good to see you," he said, and kissed her forehead.

"It's good to see you too, Jimmy," Lauryn said softly.

"How have you being doing, Rae?"

She took a deep breath and smiled. "I've been awesome. I've been working at *The Bahamas Times* as their sports reporter."

Jimmy nodded. "That's good to hear, baby girl. I have missed you so much. I know you've hung up your sprints, but you can still come and visit an old man."

Lauryn looked around, and then straight at Jimmy. She studied his face, realizing he didn't look like someone who was celebrating his 65th birthday in three months. He easily could pass for someone ten years younger. "I will try and do better."

She stopped when she saw Shannon coming towards her and Jimmy.

"Look, Jimmy, I have to go, but I'll make sure to call you. Better yet, I'll come by to see you this weekend."

Just as Shannon approached Jimmy, Lauryn leaned up and kissed him on his cheek before disappearing like a thief in the night. Jimmy listened to Shannon, but it fell upon deaf ears; Jimmy was too busy trying to figure out what the hell had happened between those two.

***

Lauryn went looking for Mia; she wasn't surprised to find her right up under Malik, and they were heading for the exit. She looked around and saw Kenyon, giving him a million dollar smile. "Cat got your tongue, Kenyon? Awesome race, by the way, baby," she said playfully.

Kenyon moved toward Lauryn and didn't say anything. He'd let his lips do the talking. He leaned in and kissed her. The kiss only lasted for a second, but it was filled with passion.

"No, you got my tongue, and thanks. You did an awesome job, by the way," he said, rubbing her forearm. She gave a tiny sigh because her arm was still hurting. "What happened, baby?" he asked with concern in his voice.

She looked up and replied, "Nothing, Champ, I'm fine."

Kenyon looked at her, but he didn't say anything; he knew she was lying. He kissed her forehead. "Okay, let's go and get something to eat."

Lauryn frowned. She hated the fact that she was lying to Kenyon.

When they got to her car, Lauryn noticed her back tire was out. "Damn, Ken, my tire."

. "Don't worry about it, baby. Get the spare."

Lauryn opened up the car trunk. It didn't take Kenyon long to change the tire. He put the tire in the back of his trunk. "Don't worry about buying a new tire. I'll get you one on Monday," he said, and closed the trunk.

Lauryn knew it didn't make sense to tell him that she would buy her own tire because she was only going to lose that argument. "Okay, Ken. Where do you want to go for something to eat? Or we can hang out at my house," she asked, while trying to start up her car.

"We could hang out at your house, and I'll stop for something to eat. I'm feeling some nice greasy chicken shack," Kenyon said with a smile.

"I'm feeling you, baby," she said. She attempted to start her car again, but it wouldn't turn over.

"Pop the hood and let me see what's wrong with your car. The battery might be dead, or it might need a jump." Kenyon was happy his grandfather had taught him a little something about cars.

"Do I need a jump or what?"

He smiled. "Yes, you need a jump, Lauryn. It's a good thing your man is always prepared. I have jumper cables in the truck."

Lauryn smiled, but she was thinking it was a little too weird that her tire needed to be changed and her car needed a jump.

She silently thought, "Shannon." He had something to do with it.

Speaking of the devil, she saw him coming towards them. "Hey, do you need any help?"

"No, I'm finishing up right now, Shannon," Kenyon said, not taking his eyes off of Lauryn. She could hear the annoyance in Kenyon's voice.

"Sweetheart, can you drive a stick shift?" he asked.

Before Lauryn could answer the question, Shannon answered, "Yes, she can drive a stick shift, because I taught her."

Lauryn gave him a side glance and cut her eyes. "Shannon, he didn't ask your ass shit. He was speaking to me, thank you," she said, narrowing her eyes as she turned her attention back to Kenyon.

"Yes, I know how to drive a stick shift. Why?"

He led her over to his truck and set her up, adjusting the seat for her short legs. "I want you to drive my truck, and I will follow you because I don't know what's wrong with your car. So, to be on the safe side, just drive my truck," he said, and kissed her.

"Lauryn, I'm not done talking to your ass. Where in the hell do you think you're going?!" Shannon shouted.

Kenyon quickly turned around and walked over to Shannon. "Who the fuck do you think you're talking to?! Get it together, and fast, because your ass is writing a check you can't cash."

Lauryn loosened her seatbelt and jumped down, grabbing Kenyon's arm. "Ken, calm down, please," she begged.

"You better listen to my girl, Mr. Champ."

Lauryn interrupted what Shannon was about to say. "I am not your freaking girl! We broke up. What part of that don't you understand?!" she shouted, and spat out something in Spanish.

Kenyon didn't say anything as he looked at Shannon. "You better be careful; don't let this look fool you. I have no problem messing your little ass up. Tell those little damn people in your head to stop selling you dreams that Rae is your girl."

Kenyon pulled Rae and headed back to the truck, leaving Shannon standing in the parking lot.

Shannon stood there and watched as they drove off.

"Rae, your ass is mine…"

Chapter 15

Lauryn got home in record time, took a long hot shower, and came downstairs. She heard the doorbell and knew it was Kenyon.

"I changed my mind about the whole chicken shack and got pizza. I hope you like extra cheese," he said, and kissed her on the cheek.

"I love extra cheese. I'm going to grab something upstairs."

Kenyon placed the pizza box on the table in the family room. He got comfortable by kicking off his tennis shoes. This was not his first time in the family room, but this was the first time he actually took the time to look around and notice the décor and pictures.

In Kenyon's opinion, he thought the room was very chic. The wall was painted in burnt orange accented with dark brown, with a 52 inch flat screen TV on the wall. On each side of the TV were two double shelves filled with DVDs, along with a group photo of Lauryn and her family on the wall. There were also single shots of each member of the family in black and white placed throughout the room. A long leather couch that could comfortably seat about six people, and two love seats, were placed in the center of the room, while in the east corner, there was a fully stocked bar and three barstools which led out to the porch.

Lauryn came in from the kitchen with two plates and a beer. Kenyon got up to help with the items.

"How did you know I drink this type of beer?" He asked as they took their seat.

"Well, there was a time I was training, and I knew this was the only type of beer you could get away with drinking," she said, taking a bite of her pizza.

Kenyon shook his head. "You're so right, mama."

They sat in a comfortable silence for a while. The only sound that was heard in the room was the air-conditioner.

Kenyon looked over at Lauryn and studied her expression. How could someone so beautiful be in so much pain? He didn't care what anyone said; he knew she was over Shannon, but she wasn't over what he did to her. For a split second, Kenyon's mind went back to the conversation he and his mother had earlier. He knew he had to ask Lauryn about what happened between her and Shannon. He needed to know what the fuck was up, because Shannon was all bark with no bite. He knew it was now or never.

Lauryn sat there, her mind replaying the events of what happened earlier between herself, Shannon, and Kenyon. She knew she would have to tell Kenyon and, most importantly, her parents the truth about what happened in Texas a year and a half ago. Each and every time she looked at her body naked in the mirror, she saw the marks he left on her stomach. She also thought about how she had a miscarriage due to his anger.

He saw that she was thinking about something. Whatever it was, it was frustrating her.

Kenyon pulled Lauryn closer to him and dropped a kiss on her forehead. "What is on your mind, Rae?"

She looked at the man she loved so dearly and decided that she was not going to lie to him anymore.

"My mind was on what happened today at the stadium, and how Shannon acted like a total jackass pass ass."

Kenyon chuckled at her statement. "Don't worry about Shannon. He is a little boy trying to be a man. But, can I ask you something, sweetie?"

She took a long, deep breath and looked up into his eyes. "Sure, Ken, what did you want to ask me?"

In a quick breath, he asked, "Why did you and Shannon break up?"

Lauryn felt the tears building. Kenyon asked the question she had been dreading to answer for the last year and a half. The question she always lied about. At that moment, she had to get her thoughts together before she started answering. "Shannon and I broke up because he physically and mentally abused me for most of the four and a half years of our relationship."

"Did he try to force himself on you?"

"He tried once, but I bit his jaw," she answered.

"How did you two start dating?"

Lauryn took a deep breath, held it, and then she breathed out slowly. She knew she would have to tell him from the first time he hit her, and about what happened today when he tried to come on to her. "Shannon and I started dating shortly after I turned fourteen, and he was sixteen going on seventeen. He actually was the one who approached me first; I had just won my race, and there was an attraction between us, so we hit it off instantly."

"Was he also running track at the time?" Kenyon inquired when Lauryn went quiet on him.

"Yes, he was running at the time. He had just participated in his first Pan-American game. He also set a record in the 200 meters: 21.00 seconds flat."

"When was first time he hit you, Rae?" He lifted her on to his lap, and she turned around to face him.

"The first time he hit me was a week after my 16th birthday. He claimed that I disrespected him by dancing with other guys at my party. I remembered him being upset and leaving, and I didn't hear from him for a week or so. To my surprise, he came and picked me up for school, and we went to the beach. That's when he slapped me. After that, he promised me that he would never hit me again.

"After that, he didn't hit me anymore for six months, but he started the mental abuse. When we were in college, he became more physically abusive towards me," Lauryn continued.

"Were you two sleeping together at the time?" he asked.

"Yeah, by that time we were having sex. I was sixteen when I lost my virginity to him. I never really enjoyed sex with him because he often made me feel like I was dirty. I knew he was having sex with other girls, though. I was pregnant by him, but I had a miscarriage due to his anger."

Kenyon couldn't say anything. He couldn't believe that Lauryn had lost a child due to Shannon's bullshit. He placed his hand on her stomach and made a silent vow that the next child Lauryn carried was going to be his, and he was going to spoil her. "Who all knew you were pregnant?"

"Only Jonathan, because he was experiencing most of my morning sickness," she laughed "It's a twin thing."

Kenyon was shocked that Renee and Mia didn't know; they were so close.

"When did you finally decide to leave him?"

"I finally decided to leave when Shannon beat my ass all over my apartment because one of the guys in my study group was feeling sick and was asleep in my bed. Cole was so sick I had to call his roommate, Carmon, to come and get him. I didn't know Shannon was watching the whole time.

"When Cole and Carmon left, Shannon came, and I knew the second he entered my room that he was upset. He didn't speak at all, he just started hitting me," she said as the tears started flowing.

"He was calling me all kinds of nasty things; he told me I was a horny bitch, I'm not worth shit, a nasty bitch, and then he spit on me. I laid there and cried for Lord knows how long. Then I picked up my phone and called Jonathan to come for me."

She wiped the tears before she continued. "Jonathan and Tayshaun were in Texas the next afternoon. When I saw my brother,

I saw all the pain and anger he was in, especially when he found out that Shannon left me like that."

Lauryn lifted up her shirt and showed him the scar that ran from the right side to the left side of her stomach. Kenyon placed his hand on her stomach, and anger washed over him. "Rae, baby, I am so sorry. I didn't know he hurt you this bad," he whispered. Kenyon had seen the scars the few times they made love, but he hadn't wanted to push the issue.

"Baby, don't apologize for what he did; only Shannon can do that. I'm about to tell you something, but you have to promise me that you won't fly off the handle."

Kenyon arched his eyebrow. "Okay, mama, I promise I won't fly off the handle," he promised, and gave her a kiss.

She told Kenyon about what had happened earlier that day at the stadium between her and Shannon. Lauryn could see he was getting angry as she told him about the incident.

"I'm going kill him!"

"No, you are not, Ken. If you love me as much as I love you, you will not go after Shannon; he's not worth it."

Then she realized that by admitting everything to him, she knew she was in love with Kenyon.

Oh, damn.

Kenyon looked at Lauryn. *She loves me,* he thought. She actually loved him. Just like he loved her.

"Okay, baby, I will not go after Shannon, but if he comes near you again, please let me know. Also, you need to tell your siblings and your parents."

She kissed him on his lips. "I will let them know, Mr. Carter, only if you are there with me when I do."

Kenyon smiled. "No problem, baby. So, you are in love with me?"

Lauryn smiled. "You can say that, baby. Do you love me?"

"I have been in love with you since the fourth grade. Even when I was away in North Carolina, I was in love with you. Now I am going to show you how much I love you."

Lauryn wrapped her arms around Kenyon's neck. "Please show me."

Kenyon shifted Lauryn onto her back. "I will show you, alright," he whispered. "I love you, Rae." He leaned in and kissed Lauryn with passion. His tongue entered her mouth on impact as he swept it over Lauryn's lips.

Lauryn's eyes fluttered shut. Sweet Jesus, help her. She felt his hard erection bulging against her, and her nipples grew hard. Hell, everything was hot and on fire.

"Look at me," he whispered.

Lauryn opened her eyes. Kenyon gazed into her eyes, feeling nothing but passion and fire. He undid her ponytail, watching her hair fall as he ran his fingers through it. Their kiss became longer, and he started nibbling and placing butterfly kisses along her neck. Lauryn knew she was going to have one hell of a passion mark. Her nipples bloomed on his tongue, and she responded by moaning softly. He moved over to the other breast, giving it equal attention.

She raked her nails over his back as Kenyon looked down at Lauryn and smiled. He brushed a soft kiss on her lips, then touched the scar on her stomach. "Let's take this party to your bedroom."

"Yes, my parents are gone for the weekend," she said, and gave him a smile.

"Music to my ears." They got up and headed towards her bedroom. When they got inside, he didn't waste any time getting their clothes off. He kissed her entire body, which Kenyon thought was so perfect. With that, he kissed her stomach, then moved down to her treasure box.

"Kenyonnnnnnnnnnnn!" she shouted as an orgasm went shooting through her body.

Kenyon came back up and kissed her; he wanted her to taste herself. "Mmmm, I taste good," Lauryn whispered.

He smiled and looked down at her. "Yes, you do, baby. Come on, we have some work to do." With that, he grabbed a condom from under the pillow where he had placed it when they first entered the room. He placed it on his shaft and entered her with one quick thrust. Now he was the one shouting her name and speaking different languages.

"Lauryn, come for me one more time," he whispered in her ear as he picked up speed with each thrust. He felt it when her treasure box grabbed his shaft, and with that, he was losing control. It sent shockwaves throughout his body; Kenyon rolled off of her and gave them a minute to catch their breaths. He pulled her closer and kissed her forehead.

"That was amazing, baby," Lauryn said as she made small circles on his chest. "Can we go for round two, please? This time, I'll be on to," she stated.

Kenyon laughed. "Baby, you don't have to ask; this body belong to you. So come on."

Lauryn didn't have to be told twice as she climbed on top and slid down on his shaft slowly. She picked up speed while arching her back. Kenyon moved his hands all across her body, leaning up to suck on her breasts, then moved his hand to her treasure box, which he knew she was enjoying. She arched her back a little more before she screamed out his name one last time and collapsed on his chest.

"I love you so much, baby."

Chapter 16

Lauryn glanced around the room. Her father sat in his favorite chair, her mother was next to him, Ryan was on the sofa with Lena's feet in his lap, and Quentin and Jonathan were sitting by the bar.

"Okay, Rae, what do you have to tell us that's so important?" Max asked, taking a sip of his drink and not taking his eyes off of Kenyon.

Lauryn knew her what her father was thinking. "No, Daddy, I'm not pregnant."

She heard sighs of relief going throughout the room. "I asked you all to come because I wanted tell you the truth about why Shannon and I broke up." Lauryn took a deep breath and looked over at Kenyon, then she started to tell her family the same story that she told Kenyon a few days ago.

Her father and brothers sprung out of their chairs like cats. Max spoke first. "I am going kill his little ass tonight," he said angrily.

"I am going to kill that motherfucker, too," Ryan yelled in rage.

"I want his bitch ass now," Quentin also shouted.

"We all want his bitch ass now, and we'll leave his ass with a scar like he left Rae," Jonathan said.

"What damn scar?" her brothers and father yelled in unison.

"Oh, shit, sorry, Rae."

Lauryn raised up her shirt. "This scar," she said.

Her mother came to her side and started to cry. "Baby, why didn't you tell anyone?"

Lauryn started to cry. "I don't know, Mommy. I feel so stupid for not saying something sooner," she said, wiping away her tears.

Angelica shook her head. "No, Rae you're not stupid. You were just scared."

Max interjected. "I don't want you be scared anymore. If his little ass comes near you, or he calls you, Rae, call me or Tay."

"Or you can call of us," Quentin said, and kissed her forehead.

Lena spoke for the first time that night. "Rae, don't call these jackasses. Do what Daddy say and call him or Tay."

Lauryn knew better then to call her brothers, or Kenyon, because she knew for a fact that they would kill Shannon and get real comfortable in Fox Hill. One thing she didn't want was anyone getting in trouble on account of her, especially her brothers and the man she loved.

Lauryn looked at Kenyon and smiled. She could already see him in a black tux on their wedding day. She could also see her belly swollen with his child.

Why in the hell am I thinking about our wedding day and being pregnant?

***

Kenyon knew for a fact that it took a lot out of Lauryn to tell her parents and brothers what happened. Now that the hard part was over, it was time for the real work to begin, and that was to get Lauryn back on the track so she could win a gold medal alongside him. He didn't want them just to win a gold medal together, but also get married and have children together. He could already see her walking down the aisle in a beautiful white dress on her father's arm. He could also see a swollen belly with their child. Where in the hell did those thoughts come from?

***

Lauryn lay in her bed and thought about how happy she was for the first time in a long time. After that night, Kenyon and Lauryn started hanging out more. She spent most weekends with him, and the sex was amazing. She was happy that she had got an IUD in place after her miscarriage, because a few times the two of them had gotten out of hand, and neither one of them remembered using a condom. Kenyon was freaking out at first, but she assured him that she was on birth control.

Kenyon called every morning before he went to the track. He brought her lunch before he went to work, and most nights, if they weren't hanging out, they talked on the phone for hours. Secretly, Lauryn knew that her mother was hoping that she and Kenyon worked out, because she started referring to him as her son-in-law. She knew her father liked Kenyon, because the other night, he invited him to tag along with him, her brothers, and Tayshaun to domino night at her Uncle Timmy's house, and also when they went fishing last Sunday.

The telephone rang, breaking her thoughts. She knew for a fact that it was Renée calling. "Yes, Ren," she said.

"Come down and open the door for Mia and me," she said. Before she had time to respond, the phone line went dead.

Lauryn jumped out of her bed and headed towards the front door to greet her best friends. "Don't we look different since we started getting some?" Renée pointed out, walking through the door with a bottle of wine.

"Yes, we do look different. We're smiling and glowing," Mia said.

Lauryn rolled her eyes at her friend's statement. "Hello to you too, ladies," she said, following them to the kitchen.

"So what if we're having sex," Lauryn continued, grabbing a dish and three wine glasses to set on the breakfast counter.

"So, besides having sex, what else y'all been up to?" Renée asked.

"Let me see... falling in love with each other more and more each day," Lauryn said happily.

Mia's eyes lit up, and she said, with excitement in her voice, "Hot damn, my girl is in love."

They all laughed at Mia's statement.

"We are happy for you; I thought, after Shannon, you would not be bothered with love anymore," Renee said as she took a sip of her wine.

"Thank you, ladies. I have something to tell you two, so let's go upstairs," Lauryn said, and grabbed the bottle of wine. Mia and Renée followed behind with their wine glasses. "This sounds deep, Rae," Mia said.

The girls were all settled on Lauryn's bed, just like when they were in high school and had sleepovers.

"Okay, Rae, what do you have to tell us?" Renée asked with a worried tone.

Lauryn took a deep breath before speaking. Mia and Renée listened and did not interrupt her as she told them everything that had happened between her and Shannon. Lauryn also revealed that she was pregnant when she left for college. That was the first time she had revealed to her girls that she had been pregnant with Shannon's child. She even told them how she had miscarried after one of Shannon's heated disagreements.

Both Mia and Renée were speechless. They still couldn't believe that their best friend had been pregnant and didn't say anything. They both grabbed Lauryn's hand as they sat in silence and let their tears flow.

"I love you, girls," she whispered, laying her head on Renée's shoulder. Mia laid her head in Lauryn's lap as Lauryn started to cry.

✳✳✳

Jonathan and Kenyon gathered around the pool table at the bowling alley as Tayshaun racked the balls. For the last three weeks, the guys got together every Thursday to play pool, or to go bowling. Kenyon liked having guys' time with Taysahun and Jonathan, but he loved the time spent with Lauryn just a little bit more.

"I think I'm going ask Renée to marry me," Tayshaun said.

Both Kenyon and Jonathan stopped drinking their drinks and gave Tayshaun their undivided attention.

"What do you mean, you think you're going to ask Ren to marry you?" Kenyon asked, dumbfounded.

"I mean Ren and I have been together for the last six years, and we're practically married, just not on paper, and not living together," he said.

Jonathan gave the timeout sign. "Timeout. You want to marry Ren because you're tired of having sex in sin?"

"No, asshole, I want to marry her because I love her, and I want to make her my wife. This doesn't have anything to do with sex. Contrary to popular belief, Renée and I didn't start having sex until the third year of our relationship," he said.

Kenyon was surprised about Tayshaun's confession. They may be best friends, but kissing and telling each other's business wasn't their thing.

"Well, brother, since it's not about sex, and you love her, then ask her. I just ask that I be your best man." Kenyon said, and patted his back.

"Same here, brother, because you know she's going to have Mia and Rae as her maids of honor or whatever the hell you call them," Jonathan said, taking a sip of his beer.

Tayshaun smiled at the two men who he considered brothers. "Sure, we got a deal, gentleman."

Kenyon glanced at his phone and saw a text message from Lauryn.

Lauryn: "Champ, can you order me some wings and send them home with Jonathan, PLS. THANKS BABY!

"Hey Johnny, if I didn't know any better, I'd swear to God Rae was pregnant. She eat wings like every damn day," Kenyon laughed.

Jonathan agreed with Kenyon one hundred percent. "Tell me about it, Champ. That gal loves her some wings. You sure my sister isn't pregnant?" Jonathan asked, and gave him a sly smile.

"I don't kiss and tell, but I tell you this much: you'll know when Rae gets pregnant. You'll probably be the first to know," Kenyon said, and patted Jonathan's back.

"Don't worry. You wouldn't have to tell me; Rae just happens to be my twin, so we have a very special connection. I can usually sense what mood Rae is in," he said.

Kenyon didn't say anything for a second. "So what mood has Lauryn been in lately?"

Jonathan smiled. "My brother, you already know, but I'm still going to tell you." He took a deep breath "Rae is happy, at peace, and in love. All thanks to you, Kenyon."

Kenyon smiled at the man who was connected to the soul of the woman he loved. "You are so right, because I am feeling those things about Rae."

Tayshaun hosed back the last of his beer. "Oh, damn, now that we had our Oprah moment, let's get back to our game."

They talked about everything from sports, politics, their jobs, and local news, and later left after three more rounds.

Chapter 17

It was the last week in June; Lauryn sat at her desk and finished up the last of the layout for the special edition with the "Golden Girls" and "Golden Knights" for Derek to edit. It took Lauryn six weeks to complete, but felt like it was her best work yet. Working on this project made her realize how much she missed the track. A few times she contemplated calling Jimmy to tell him that she was ready to come back. Then she thought how unfair it would be to Kenyon, because she knew for a fact that he was working hard. She also knew how much it meant for him to make it to the World Games and the Olympics. Lauryn realized how much she wanted to win a gold medal when she interviewed Chris Brown at his home, and Kenyon had tagged along. He was like a kid in a candy store; he was hanging on every word Chris said. After they left that night, she went home and cried. With each tear, she let her fear, pain, rage, and any other negative emotion she was feeling, go.

Lauryn picked up her cell phone and texted Kenyon.

Lauryn: "Champ, I need to talk to you about something tonight."

Kenyon: "Sure, sweetie, it sounds important"

Lauryn: "Yea, it's kind of important, dear."

Kenyon: "Okay, I will pick you up round 7, and then I'll take you for some wings or ice cream or whatever you want, mama?"

Lauryn: "Cool, will you pick me up from work? Mia is coming for my car in the next hour or so. And I love the way you think, baby, with the wing thing."

Kenyon: "LOL…… I would love to see the day you can't eat wings. I will be there to pick you up around 5:30 or so. By then, the traffic should have already died down."

Lauryn: "Don't say things like that, baby; I don't even want to think about that day. LOL! :P"

Kenyon: "Love you, baby, and see you later."

Lauryn: "Love you too!"

Kenyon placed his phone back into his gym bag and smiled. He meant what he said about the day Lauryn couldn't eat wings.

"Stop daydreaming and get your red ass back on the track! Start at the 200 meter mark! You really need to work on how you adjust your body when you are running on the curve. I hate to tell you this, but you've gained close to three seconds on each curve, which means you've lost about 12 seconds. Since you know numbers so well, you figure that out while you're running on the curve," Jimmy said to Kenyon.

Kenyon was not surprised that Jimmy called him out on his inability to run on the curve. His specialty may be the 200 meter and 400 meter, but Kenyon knew God was on his side each and every time he felt his body slowing down on the curve. From the time Coach Kay coached him, he showed him what he needed to work on in terms of his body formation on the curve. And now Jimmy was preaching the same thing as Coach Kay. Kenyon knew he had to put in some extra hours to improve his ability to run on the curve.

"I got you, Jimmy," he said as he walked to the 200 meter mark. Kenyon got in position and listened for Jimmy's whistle.

Kenyon became aware of his body as he sprinted on the curve, and did just like Jimmy told him; he mentally counted how long it took to run the curve. He was adding 3.5 seconds, which was not good.

He headed over to Jimmy. "You were actually right. I calculated 3.5 seconds, and personally, I am in some deep shit. That means I'm adding a total of 14 seconds, which is uncalled for," Kenyon said.

"I do agree with you; 14 seconds is uncalled for. Your personal best is 45 seconds. I don't know how you did it, but we need to figure out how, Ken," Jimmy said, tapping his shoulder.

Kenyon agreed. "I totally agree with you."

"You need to ask Rae to give you some tips on running the curve," Jimmy said, and went back to making notes on his clipboard.

"Why?" Kenyon asked curiously.

Jimmy laughed. "Well, Champ, your girlfriend just happens to be an excellent sprinter when running on the curve; it just happens to be her specialty."

Kenyon wondered how in the hell could Lauryn could be excellent on the curve when she was only 5'1". She has short legs, so she would have to work ten times harder.

Jimmy answered the question he knew was stewing in his head. "I guess you're wondering how Rae is able to run the curve so well despite her height. After training her for more than fifteen years, I'm still unable to answer that question myself. All I can say is, only Lauryn and the good Lord can answer that question. But let me tell you a story about Rae."

Jimmy removed his glasses and headed over to the bleachers. Kenyon walked behind him and sat next to him. He wondered what this story was about as he got comfortable. "I'm all ears, Jimmy."

Jimmy sighed. "It was the 2009 Caribbean Junior Games. That was the first time the games had been held in the Bahamas in about ten years. The hype was around your girlfriend, and it was the final heat of the 100 and 200 meters. Everyone in the stadium knew that Lauryn was long overdue for one because, from day one, Rae was only doing enough to qualify for both the 100 and 200 meters. The crowd didn't care that she won gold the night before with

Brittany, Alyssa, and Simone in the 4x1 relay. As far as they were concerned, she wasn't giving her all."

"Damn," Kenyon whispered.

"I know, damn is right. But, truth be told, Rae was not giving her all because her and Shannon were arguing; I think he was also hitting her at that time. Anyway, I went looking for her to have a chat, but she found me first. She looked at me and said, 'Jimmy, I'm going to give the people of the Caribbean something to talk about for the next twenty-five years.' I asked what was she talking about, and baby girl told me without batting an eye, 'I'm going to set a CJ Game record in both the 100 and 200 meters, and my daughter, Ayanna-Joy whatever her father's last name may be, is going to be the one to beat my record,'" Jimmy said and laughed.

Kenyon smiled; he liked the name Ayanna-Joy. He could see her looking every bit like Lauryn. Actually, he liked that name a lot, since Joy was his mother's middle name.

Jimmy took a sip of his water. "Sorry about that. I don't mean to laugh every time I tell this story, because Rae was completely serious. So, like I was saying, my girl laced up her sprints for the 100 meters, and they placed her in lane eight. The reporters were already saying that Jamaica's Kim Ross was going to get the gold, St. Lucia's Lee-Anna Spencer the silver, and it would be between Bermuda's Brandi Brown and Rae to get the bronze. Your girlfriend took that to prediction to heart; she got in the blocks and looked over at her father, Max, and we both said, 'Gold!'"

"When that gun fired, Rae came out of those blocks with fire, and when she crossed the finish line, she kissed and waved at the crowed stadium. When the announcer said that she was beating her own record of 10.70, and had set a new record of 10.65, the stadium went in a uproar."

"I could imagine, Jimmy, and, knowing Rae, she just ate that attention up," Kenyon said happily.

"You know your girlfriend all too well. About an hour later, it was time for the 200 meter, and the reporters and everyone was wondering if lightning was going to strike twice. She did it, clocking in at 22.77. The stadium was in an uproar again, as if it was like

Boxing Day morning. When I went over to hug her, I saw something in Rae's eyes that I thought would never die."

"What did you see?" Kenyon asked softly.

"I saw her passion for life, and for the track. Kenyon, I told you this story because I know you will help her get that passion back. You love her."

Kenyon smiled. "Yes, I do love her, and I will do anything to help her get that passion back." He got up and gave Jimmy a bear hug.

"I know you will, Ken. See you in the morning with my coffee, thank you very much."

He waved his hand because he knew Jimmy needed his coffee to get his day started, just like he did. Until he won his gold medal, though, there would be no caffeine in his system. At first it was hard to get used to drinking tea, but after the first few weeks, he'd adjusted.

Ken glanced at his watch, knowing he needed a shower, and get over to the office, and then to pick up Lauryn later. He was really curious about what she wanted to talk about. He hoped that whatever it was, it didn't have anything to with Shannon. He was really not in the mood since Lauryn has come clean about what happened between the two. Her spunk had come back, and her big brown eyes were brighter than ever. Kenyon was glad that he had something to do with it. He was hoping that spunk and those bright eyes would never die.

Chapter 18

Lauryn was editing "Potcake Says," the weekly column that had been written for the las fifty years by the same man, William 'Potcake' Rolle, when Derek came by her desk. "What are you still doing here, Lauryn?" he asked, looking at his watch.

She gave a sweet smile. "Mia has my car, and I'm waiting for my boyfriend to pick me up,"

Derek was not surprised by Lauryn's statement about having a boyfriend. He'd heard the office gossip about how he brought her lunch on most days, and he was also training for the World Games, and that he was Bobby Carter's grandson. "Oh, your boyfriend is picking you up. I see."

Lauryn rolled her eyes; she knew the office gossip about her relationship with Kenyon was in high gear. Especially since he always bringing her lunch. Also, there was a picture of them that she took in her office, and Gossip Queen LaTonya saw them out a few times. Derek loved good office gossip just a little more than the women, despite the fact that he was always preaching that all office gossip should be kept to a minimum.

"Yes, my boyfriend is picking me up. I don't know why you're playing crazy. I know for a fact the whole office is talking about it."

He laughed. "I have nothing to say; you're a grown woman, Rae, but I will tell you this much. You seem happier and, as a result, your writing has gotten better. I'm not saying that your writing wasn't good before, but now it's at a whole new level."

Lauryn smiled because Derek didn't often give compliments. When he did, she had to take that to heart. "Thanks, Derek!"

He took a deep breath. "Now, don't run and tell everyone I'm in the business of giving out kudos, okay?"

She laughed. "Don't worry, your secret is safe with me."

Her cell phone rang, and it was Kenyon's ring tone. "Excuse me, I have to get this."

"That's okay, Rae. I'll see you tomorrow."

She answered her phone. "I'm going to be down in five minutes, baby. No, I don't need you to come and get me. Yes, I'm sure."

Lauryn grabbed her bag and headed downstairs. When she got outside, Kenyon was parked out front and playing with his cell phone. She smiled, because he always playing with his phone. She jumped in the truck and gave him a kiss on the lips. "Good afternoon, Rae."

"Good afternoon to you too, Ken," she said happily.

He put the truck in gear, and there was a comfortable silence between them. Lauryn's mind was going into overdrive as she got her thoughts together. She knew that Kenyon was going to support whatever she did, but she was also scared to tell him. Lauryn didn't want him to feel like she was raining on his parade, because she knew how important winning a gold medal was to him.

Kenyon glanced over at Lauryn and could tell that whatever she had to tell him, it really had to been big. She wouldn't even look at him as she stared out the window.

He couldn't figure out what she had to say. "Okay, Rae, baby, what's so important that you had to tell me?" he asked without taking his eyes off the road.

She smiled at him. "I'll tell you once you feed me some wings."

Kenyon laughed and put his hand on her thigh. "Oh, I have to feed you to get an answer, Lauryn Rae? That's how you're going to play your man?"

"Yes!" she said happily.

"That's fine with me. We could just fly to get your wings. Why is Mia driving your car?"

"Hers is in the shop. I believe it's getting service," she told him.

"Oh, okay. I didn't know Mia was allowed to drive anyone's car."

Lauryn laughed; she knew where he was going with that statement. "Mia is allowed to drive anyone's car except Renée's.

Mind you, Mia is an excellent driver; Que taught her how to drive when she was fourteen.

"Not bad at all. Since you have something to tell me, I need you to help me with something," Kenyon said, pulling into the parking space.

He gave her a kiss on her cheek and smiled. "But I'll tell you once we're inside."

Lauryn nodded, wondering what he needed help with.

The two grabbed their usual table on the deck overlooking the beach and placed their order. Both of them were in deep thought, and had an uncomfortable silence for about ten minutes before they both realized they had something to say.

She looked at Kenyon and took a deep breath.

Kenyon smiled inwardly because he thought she looked so sexy. He grabbed her hand and gave a soft smile, allowing her to know that whatever she had to tell, she could. "Okay, Beauty, what's on your mind?"

"Champ, I miss the track. I'm ready to take control of my life, starting with me running track again. But, Ken..." Lauryn stopped and started to look away.

Kenyon waited for a few seconds to see if she would continue. He knew it took a lot out of her to tell him that she missed the track. Kenyon also knew how Shannon made her give up track because he had his own childish insecurities.

He watched her closely as she got her thoughts together. He grabbed her hand and rubbed it softly. "Breathe, and tell me what else is on your mind," he said softly.

Lauryn could feel the tears building up because she was scared to go any further. She didn't want Kenyon to feel like she was taking away his spotlight. She knew how important winning a gold medal at the World Games and the Olympics was to him. When the first tear rolled down her face, it hit her that Kenyon was nothing like Shannon, so no matter what, he was going to support her.

"Kenyon, baby, I don't want you to feel like I'm stealing your spotlight. I know how much winning the gold medal means to you, and if you feel like I will be, then please let me know now."

Kenyon's anger was building up; he couldn't believe that Lauryn was willing to put her goals on hold because she feared that she was taking away his spotlight. He knew Shannon was the reason she was acting this way. She would indirectly hold back in races, or if he was around, she tried to limit the interview.

He put his hands up to wipe away her tears. "Listen to me, Lauryn Rae Smith. I don't want you to ever feel like you have to put your dreams on hold to please me. Your victory is my victory, and my victory is yours. As long as I have breath in my body, I don't want to hear you talking about you taking a backseat on anything. I only want you to ride shotgun, sweetheart. I love you, girl," Kenyon said, and gave her a kiss.

Lauryn laughed and smiled. "I got the message, Kenyon, and I love you too."

He sweetly smiled and kissed her again. "I love you too, Lauryn."

Kenyon smiled. He loved her so much. He wanted to erase the last eight years of her life, which had been filled with so much pain and hurt. More than anything, he wanted to slap the shit out of Shannon for all the hell he had put her through.

He laughed as she took a sip of her drink and a bite of her wing. If she wanted to get back on the track, she needed to ease up on her wing obsession.

Kenyon grabbed her wing before speaking. "Baby, you do realize that you're going to have to ease up on your wing obsession."

Lauryn finished chewing her food. "Please don't remind me. I could do it(,) but I do need to find someone to train me since Jimmy is training you now," she said.

"True, but you know better than anyone that Jimmy would work something out with you. Also, I know Jimmy wouldn't mind training you. He wants you to get back on the track."

Lauryn rolled her eyes because she knew Kenyon was right. Besides, the two years she was away at college, Jimmy had been her only coach. She also knew that any coach in the country would be thrilled to train her, even though she hadn't laced her sprints up in eighteen months.

"You know me all too well, Champ, but I took a personal day tomorrow so I could go down to the track and have a talk with Jimmy," Lauryn said happily.

Kenyon was happy to hear that she took a personal day, because if he could get to the track early, she could help him with his curve issue. "I like the sound of that. Why don't you come to workout and practice with me so, that way, you could help me with my problem."

She arched her eyebrow. She forgot he needed her help with something. "I'll think about it. What do you need help with, anyway?"

"Jimmy told me that I need to work on my deliver on the curve, and from my understanding, my love, you're excellent on the curve, Kenyon said, and kissed the end of her nose.

Lauryn giggled. "Oh, yes, Champ, you need to work on your deliver. I don't know how in the hell you managed to win your races. But don't worry, I will help you tomorrow; that means you have to get your ass up a little earlier to get me."

"Well, you could sleep half an hour later if we have a sleepover," he said.

"Okay, cool. I just need to go home to get my sprints and workout clothes. I don't have any over at your place." Since they had started dating, he told her that she could leave some of her stuff at his place.

Kenyon paid the bill, and they left. Halfway through the ride, Kenyon noticed that her head was lying awkward, which meant she was sleep. He thought, even while she was asleep, she still looked beautiful.

His thoughts continued as he pictured her in a white gown wearing a bright smile as she crossed the finish line in Sydney.

Chapter 19

Jimmy turned on the light in the treatment room and was greeted by Lauryn sleeping on her right side; her head was resting on her hands while her legs were pulled into the fetal position. He smiled, remembering all the times, when they'd first built the training site, that he would find her either sleeping in here or in his office when she had early morning workouts. Jimmy was happy to see her, so he gave a silent prayer.

***

It was seven in the morning, and Lauryn was like a mad woman without her coffee. She and Kenyon arrived at the track shortly after five. She had never been a morning person, even when she was in training, so it was hell for her to get up without coffee, especially since she couldn't have it.

"I need my damn coffee," she mumbled under her breath as she went to look for Kenyon.

She walked down the hall towards the workout room. She stopped to look at the wall, only to see pictures of herself, the Sand twins, Chris Brown, Vincent Thompson, and the one of her Alyssa, Brittany, and Simone when they both won Under 17 and Under 20.

Lauryn especially looked at the one of her at the CJ Games in 2009. That's when she realized how much she really missed track and was ready to get back into the sport. For a split second she saw herself crossing the finish line at the Olympics, and Kenyon was there cheering her on.

"I'm ready," she said to herself.

Lauryn walked into the workout room and saw Kenyon was already there. He smiled as he placed the weight on the rack and walked over to her. "Good morning, Sleeping Beauty," he said, brushing a kiss on her forehead. Lauryn closed her eyes and rested her head on his chest.

"Morning, baby. I really need some coffee."

Kenyon laughed. "No, you don't. Why don't you drink some of my tea?"

"I don't drink tea, Kenyon. I want coffee now," she whined.

He shook his head and got his keys from his bag. "Here, brat, bring me back a bottle of orange juice, an egg omelet, and toast."

Lauryn took the keys and money from him, and gave him a kiss on his cheek. "No problem, baby. I'm a brat only when I don't get my coffee."

Kenyon playfully slapped her bottom. "Whatever you say, brat," he said.

***

"Where is Rae?" Jimmy asked as Kenyon made his way over to the track.

"The brat went to get coffee and OJ."

Jimmy just shook his head. Lauryn had been a coffee drinker from the time she was ten. Against her mother's wishes, of course, but her father and Quentin would sneak in and give her coffee. Once she started training, she was back to sneaking coffee because Jimmy told her she either gave up her wing obsession, or she gave up coffee.

"She better enjoy her coffee; if she gets back on the track, it's either her wing obsession or coffee. One has to go."

Kenyon burst out laughing. "I'll have to get Rae pregnant for her to give up her wings obsession and coffee. Did you know she eats wings every day?"

Jimmy smiled. "Shit, I know all too well that she eats wings every day. And you'd better not be getting her pregnant, or you two will be sharing the same last name."

"Yes, sir, I will keep that in mind."

"Good, now go and run five laps for me."

Kenyon stretched and started his laps. He liked running laps because it allowed him to think clearly. Right now, the only thing that was on his mind was Lauryn, and winning a gold medal, but Lauryn a little more. He was debating for the longest time whether or not he should ask her to marry him. More than anything, Kenyon wanted her to be happy.

A few nights ago, he'd had a heart to heart with her mother. When he went to pick Lauryn up for their date and arrived early, Angelica had used that time to her advantage…

"Ken, I'm not going to read the riot act because I know my husband and sons already did. The fact that you got her to tell us about what happened between her and Shannon says a lot about your character, and how my daughter feels about you. She has loved you since the fourth grade."

His facial expression was priceless. "Yes, since the fourth grade. All I ask of you is to get married and give me some grandbabies. Most of all, get her little ass back on the track."

Kenyon laughed. "I will do everything in my power to get her back on the track."

"Well, damn, you went all the way to China for this damn coffee?" Jimmy asked as Lauryn approached him with a cup of coffee.

She laughed. "No, I didn't." Jimmy sipped his coffee and shook his head. "Hurry up and eat; we need to a have chat."

Lauryn nodded and started to eat hot grits and tuna. As she ate, she watched Kenyon closely and made mental notes along the way. Even though he was only doing laps, Kenyon had a nasty form, mainly when he was on the curves. "That's not going to work," she mumbled to herself.

"Okay, baby girl, talk to me?"

She put her breakfast aside and gave her undivided attention. "Jimmy, I'm ready. I need to get back on track." She took a breath. "But there's something I need to tell you first."

Jimmy knew what she had to tell him; he already knew what had happened between her and Shannon. The night Lauryn called Jonathan and Tayshaun to come and get her, they told him what was going on just in case things got a little wild. He promised them that he was not going to say anything. He was a man of his word.

He put his hand up and stopped her before she continued. "Baby girl, you don't have to tell me anything," he said, kissing her on check.

Lauryn arched her eyebrow. "What in the hell do you mean, I don't have to tell you anything? That damn Kenyon talks so much."

"Let's get something straight, Lauryn; Kenyon did not say a damn thing to me. That boy fears you like he fears God. Also, he loves you too much to break your trust. So are we clear?"

"Crystal!"

"Good, now let's go and see what you have left in the tank," he said, kissing her on the cheek again.

It was shortly after two when they called it a day. Despite not being on the track in more than a year, Lauryn thought for sure she would have been sore. To her surprise, she felt like she had been working out every day. She headed over to the bleachers where Jimmy was talking with Jasmine and Kenyon.

"You look good out there, Beauty," Kenyon said. He pulled her on his lap and gave her a kiss on the lips. She giggled and kissed him back. "Thank you, baby," she said, kissing him again.

"Cut that shit out," Jimmy said.

They both laughed. "What can I say, Jimmy? I love to kiss my baby," Kenyon said, kissing her once again.

Jimmy just shook his head; he'd never seen her so happy. When she was with Shannon, either Lauryn was either in distress or annoyed, but mostly unhappy. It was as if Shannon was slowly killing her soul. One thing Jimmy learned about Lauryn was that her inner beauty always outshined her outer beauty. He was glad Kenyon realized that, because he knew Lauryn's inner beauty was front and center.

"Baby girl, you look good out there. You would never know you haven't worked out in months. With that being said, I'm willing to work with your schedule for the workouts. It's not going to be easy, but one thing I know is that you can pull it off."

Lauryn moved from Kenyon's lap to give Jimmy a hug and a kiss. She knew, deep down, no matter what, Jimmy would help her.

"Thanks you so much, Jimmy! I love you."

"You're most welcome, baby girl. I'll see you tomorrow, bright and early," Jimmy said to Lauryn as he kissed her forehead. "As for you, Champ, I don't want to see your red Long Island ass around this track until Monday, understand?" he said, looking over his sunglasses at Kenyon.

Kenyon laughed. "Yes, sir, I do."

"Good, now get your asses out of here. I'm a busy man."

Lauryn and Kenyon laughed and walked hand in hand. They hit the showers, then left and went over to his house, where she made lunch. Then they snuggled up on the sofa to watch *Iron Man 3*. Before they knew it, they were fast asleep.

Chapter 20

Lauryn was at peace for the first time in a long time. Based on the schedule she and Jimmy had worked out, she was on the track six days of the week: Tuesday, Wednesday, Thursday, and Friday she would work out from 4 am to 6am, and then she would go over to her grandmother's house to get ready for work. Then she would return from 5 PM to 8 PM. For Saturdays, her schedule was from 6 AM to 1PM, and Sundays, her schedule was from 4 PM to 7 PM.

Kenyon was with her every step of the way. He made sure she ate, got enough rest, and iced her body. Her mother asked if she moved in with Kenyon, since she was always there. Since she started training, Lauryn may have slept at home twice.

Lauryn knew how blessed she was to have Kenyon in her life. Now, everything was going in the right direction. She was falling in love with Kenyon more each day. She was also getting her passion back for track. She was becoming a better person. Hell, she was even becoming a better woman.

Lauryn glanced at her watch and realized she was running late for practice with Jimmy. She picked the office phone up and called him. After the third ring, he answered

"Lauryn Rae, your ass better be here in twenty minutes. If not, your ass will be running laps until you and Kenyon have children."

She laughed, "I will be there in 15, and I will bring a three for five. Love you, Jimmy."

"Selling me a three for five will not work. Just bring your ass, and see in you fifteen minutes. Love you too, baby girl."

Lauryn hung up the phone and started to shut down her computer.

***

Shannon jumped out of his car, crossed the parking lot of *The Bahamas Times,* and headed over to Lauryn's car. He walked up behind her and said softly, "Lauryn, baby, we need to stop meeting like this in the parking lot."

Lauryn froze as soon as she heard his voice. "Shannon, what do you want?" She cringed when ~~he~~ his hands touched her.

"I want you, Rae; all of you," he said, rubbing the nape of her neck. Lauryn closed her eyes as she fought back tears.

She turned and faced him before speaking. "Shannon, what you and I had was nothing but pure hell. You beat my ass everyday. Through all the bullshit you have put me through, you have yet to say to me, 'I'm sorry, Rae,' even once. One of these days I'm really going to call the police on your ass. My father isn't just the Commissioner of Police to collect a paycheck. Maybe it'll teach motherfuckers like you a lesson in messing with people. I'm tired of allowing you to control my life, so you know what, motherfucker? Go ahead and hit me. Just make sure when you're done, you can call the undertaker so he can fit your ass for your coffin," Lauryn said in one breath.

Shannon pushed up her against her car. "You think you're some big bad bitch because your daddy is the Commissioner, and your little sissy ass boyfriend wanna always fight someone. Guess what? For punk ass bitches like them, I have people like them on my payroll.

"As for me telling you sorry, I, Shannon Michael Knowles, don't tell nasty stuck-up bitches like you sorry for nothing. If anything, you should be telling me sorry. I subjected myself to four and a half years with you, and you could not please me. That's why I used to step out on your ass; that's why I used to beat your ass for breakfast, lunch, and dinner.

"As for me going to the undertaker for my coffin, if I were you, I'd be careful what I say to people."

Shannon grabbed her upper arm. "For once and for all, I'm going to shut your ass up, and take away those precious legs from you."

He held onto her left arm, which gave her full use of her right. Her fingers curled into a fist and she swung, hitting his left eye.

He groaned. "You little bitch!"

Before she could swing again, she felt a sharp pain hit her rib, then her left upper thigh. Shannon let her go, and she collapsed on the ground. Then he kicked her in the side before spitting in her face.

Tears were streaming down Lauryn's face when she felt the blood flowing from her right side, and her left thigh. She started to recite Psalm 23:

"The Lord is my Shepherd; I shall not want. He makes me lie down in green pastures. He leads me beside still waters. He restores my soul. He leads me in the paths of righteousness for his name's sake, ye though I walk through the valley of the shadow of death, I shall fear no evil for thou are with me your rod and staff may comfort me. You prepares a table before me in the presence of my enemies you anoint my head with oil my cup overflows. Surely

goodness and mercy all the days of my life and I shall dwell in the house of the Lord forever."

Then she blacked out.

***

Lauryn opened her eyes to the sound of machines monitoring her vitals. Turning her head slowly, she saw the IV taped to the back of her left hand. She was trying to say Kenyon's name, but why did her voice sound so hoarse?

Kenyon moved from the chair where he'd spent the last three days waiting for Lauryn to regain consciousness. He left long enough to take a shower and change his clothes in the hospital wing named after Lauryn's maternal grandfather, who was the first Bahamian Chief of Staff at the hospital. Her mother, Angelica, made sure that nurses provided him with all his meals and a place to shower, but Kenyon favored sleeping in the chair next to Lauryn's bed. He wanted to be there when she woke up.

He smiled and kissed her forehead. "Hey baby. Welcome back."

She tried to smile, but her lips were much too dry and cracked. "How many days have I missed?"

"Three." Leaning in, he kissed her cracked lips.

Her eyes fluttered. "Damn, that's long, Kenyon." Reaching up with her free hand, she combed her fingers through her hair and touched her eyebrows. Her hair was oily, and her eyebrows were thick. She sighed. "My hair needs to be washed, and my eyebrows need to be drawn on."

Kenyon got into the bed next to her and brushed her hair off her face, laughing and kissing her once again. "Your hair will have to wait until you are discharged. I will make sure your hair and nails are done, and as for your eyebrows, I'll make sure Ren or Mia bring your make-up bag."

She leaned up and kissed him again. "I will hold you to that, baby."

The two sat in silence before Lauryn started to speak. "Baby, will I be able to get back on the track?"

"Yes, you will be able to get back on the track," Kenyon said, and rubbed her forearm.

Lauryn leaned up and roughly captured his mouth. She could not remember the last time she ate, but at that moment, she didn't care. She had to taste her man's lips. He didn't oppose, and was returning the kiss with the same passion, making her realize just how much she loved him.

"Humph."

He heard the sound of someone clearing his throat, and was positive Lauryn also heard it, as well. Neither one of them were coming up for air, though. They made the decision to ignore it, hoping whoever it was would get the picture and go away.

Kenyon heard someone clear their throat a second time, and decided that the person was not getting the picture. In his eyes, that was not his damn problem, since Kenyon had no intention of releasing his woman's mouth until he was ready to. If whoever it was had a problem with it, they could leave the room.

"Kenyon, let my daughter come up for air," her father said with a deep voice.

He quickly released her and smiled, looking down at Lauryn, whose lips were swollen. He noticed that her brothers were also present in the room.

Her father came over and gave her a kiss on her forehead, followed by her brothers and Tayshaun. Jonathan held her a little longer than the others. The past three days had been nothing but pure hell for him, because he did not know whether his other half was going to live or not. He was holding a lot of discomfort. "I love you," he whispered softly.

Still hugging her twin brother, she whispered, "I love you too." She started crying as Jonathan looked up and wiped the tears away from her eyes. Just like Kenyon did earlier, he got in the bed with his sister. He held her, allowing her to cry; he also started to cry.

"How are you feeling, Princess?" Max asked his daughter.

"I'm in a little pain, but I will I live, Daddy," she said softly.

Max smiled at his daughter, who was looking more and more like his beloved wife. "Princess, I know this may be asking a lot of you, but I need you to tell us what you remember about the attack," he said softly.

She nodded her head and took deep a breath, then looked around the room at the six men who held a special part of her life.

"It was Shannon who attacked me, Daddy,"

Lauryn could feel the anger in the room the second Shannon's name left her mouth. She was so afraid to look up at them, so she just closed her eyes.

Lauryn heard the men muttering angrily about murder in English, Spanish, and French. Once everyone had calmed down, Max asked his sons, along with Kenyon, to ask Tayshaun to stay. Then two other officers by the names of Wells and Nottage, who worked at The Central Police Station, came in the room. Lauryn looked up at her father, then at Tayshaun, and they both gave her a soft smile.

Detective Wells was the first to speak. "Okay, Miss Smith, can we ask you a few questions about your attack?"

Lauryn nodded. "Okay, but please call me Lauryn."

"Fine, Lauryn it is. Do you know who attacked you?"

"Yes, my ex-boyfriend, Shannon Knowles."

"How long have you been broken up?"

"Shannon and I have not been together for more than a year and a half."

Detective Nottage spoke for the first time. "What was the reason behind your break-up?"

She took a deep breath. "The reason why Shannon and I broke up was because I was tired of his abuse, both mentally and physically."

"Have you reported any of the other times he hit you to the police, Lauryn?" Wells asked.

"No," she said softly.

"Why not, Lauryn?"

Lauryn started shaking her head. "To be honest with you, I don't know why."

She looked up at her father and started crying. "Daddy, I don't know why. I feel like an idiot." Max kissed his only daughter on the forehead and rubbed her back. "You are not an idiot. You were just afraid, that's all, Rae."

Tayshaun asked, "Are you done with questioning?"

Both men shook their heads. "No, Thompson, we have a few more questions, then we're done," Detective Wells spoke.

Lauryn took a few minutes, then got herself together and was able to go on with the questioning. They asked her a few more before they were done. It was a good thing she had a good memory, because she was able to tell them everything about the attack. When they were done, she started crying again because she felt humiliated for not saying anything sooner.

Chapter 21

The brothers and Kenyon were posted outside of Lauryn's hospital room. Ryan was the first to speak. "Shannon better pray to God that I'm going to be a father, because if not, his ass will be a dead motherfucker."

"Well, Ry, Que, Johnny, and I don't have shit to lose, so I will kill him for all of us. I don't have a damn problem becoming my so-call daddy's cellmate," Kenyon said.

Quentin stopped and asked, "Who is your father, Kenyon?"

Kenyon looked up and said coldly, "Charles "Casino" Adderely."

"Oh, shit, you are a crazy motherfucker," Jonathan said.

"Casino Adderly is your daddy? Damn!" Ryan and Quentin said together.

Kenyon did care what they thought of him after they realized who his father was. He knew one thing for sure, though; he look like his grandfather, but he sure as hell had some of Casino's dirty ways.

He was thinking hard on the promise he made to Lauryn about not going after Shannon. Lord knows his love for her was the only thing that was saving Shannon's little ass.

Kenyon looked up at her brothers for the first time since revealing who his father was. Their facial expressions said one word: disbelief. He understood why, though; his father's drug running days were legendary. Casino trafficked all throughout the Caribbean, South America, and the Eastern sea border of the United States. It was five years ago when his drug running days came to an end. He was arrested by US Federal Agents in North Carolina with cocaine, which had a street value of about 3.9 million dollars. Kenyon still believed he came to North Carolina to look for him because it was six weeks before his 18th birthday. On the day of his birthday, he received a package that held all of his father's assets, which were put in his name.

"Kenyon, are you mixed up in Casino's lifestyle?" Quentin asked.

He stopped and looked at him for a second before answering him. "Why in the hell would you ask me a question like that, Que?"

"Why do you think I asked? My sister is laid up in a hospital bed because she's mixed up with one asshole, so I have no other choice but to ask!" Quentin exclaimed, getting into Kenyon's face.

Kenyon shouted, "Get the hell out of my face!"

"What are you going to do? Call big bad Casino on me?"

Ryan pulled Quentin away. "You both need to chill! Emotions are running a little high right now. Rae wouldn't want you two acting like assholes," Ryan fumed. He looked at Quentin, who was mumbling under his breath. "Que, you know damn well Ken is not mixed up in his father's lifestyle. He loves her too much to hurt her."

He then looked over at Kenyon, who was also mumbling under his breath. "Kenyon, you can't be too upset. It's not like your father is some saint or anything. Que just needs to make sure, that's all."

Ryan looked at both men and smiled. "Now, you two kiss and make-up before I call Angelica to beat both of your asses."

Kenyon and Quentin gave each other hugs and apologized. Ryan placed his arms around them and said, "My big brother job is never done. Now, let's go check on our baby."

Lauryn remained in the hospital for five more days before she was released. She was happy her mother was a well-known doctor around the hospital, because her family and friends became fixtures around the hospital long after visiting hours were over. Especially Kenyon. Besides going to practice, he refused to leave her side. Once he had time to, he called his grandmother, Dora, to come to hospital and bring Lauryn her famous pea soup.

Jimmy also came to see her, and they had a long chat about returning to the track. That was one of the rare occasions where her parents, her brothers, Kenyon, Tayshaun, Mia, and Renée were not hovering over her. They had a nice long chat, which ended with the two in tears. She promised Jimmy the next time she hung up her sprints would be when she became pregnant. He told her to make sure it was not until after the 2016 Olympics.

Chapter 22

"Shannon Knowles, you are under arrest. Anything you say can be and will be held against you in the court of law. If you don't have a lawyer, one will be appointed to you by the crown," Wells said, placing Shannon under arrest.

"What I'm being arrested for?" Shannon asked as they placed him in the back seat of the patrol car.

"You are under arrest for the attempted murder of Lauryn Smith, Mr. Knowles. That is what you are under arrest for," he said, slamming the door.

Shannon didn't get it because, in his eyes, Lauryn caused whatever happened to her. His lawyer entered the room first, then Wells and Nottage. They gave Shannon cold looks as they sat in front of him. If Nottage didn't have the willpower he did, he would have slapped the shit out of Shannon. In his eyes, Lauryn was his new baby sister because she was so sweet.

"Look, Shannon, we don't have time for the long talk. We know you attacked Lauryn and left her to die," Nottage said, slamming his hands on the table.

Shannon gave them an evil smile and laughed. "So you say."

"You don't have any proof my client was the one who attacked Miss Smith," his lawyer said, looking over at Wells and Nottage.

"That's where you are wrong, my friend. Just before Miss Smith was attacked by your client, she called 919 and opened the line. We have the entire incident on tape, and also on hard copy." Nottage placed the tape and folder on the table in front of his attorney, then hit play on the tape recorder.

The facial expression on his attorney's face was speechless as he listened to the tape. He looked over at Shannon and started shaking his head, then whispered something in his ear. Shannon didn't say anything, but his facial expression read nothing but pure anger. Wells came over to place Shannon under arrest, and booked him for attempted murder.

Two weeks later, Shannon was brought before Magistrate Michelle Cartwright. She was not going to have mercy on him, either. She didn't care that Lauryn Smith was the daughter of the Commissioner of Police, the granddaughter of the former Chief Justice, or that she and Lauryn's mother, Angelica, served on various committees together. She knew many would say that it was ethically wrong for her to hear the case due to her personal relationship with the victim's family, but it really didn't make much of a difference; every other Magistrate on the bench knew Lauryn's family on a personal or professional level.

Lauryn sat in the gallery with her family and friends. Jonathan was on her left and Kenyon was on the right. Despite Kenyon and her brothers wanting her to stay home, Lauryn felt she needed to be there to have some closure. When Shannon entered the courtroom, he turned and gave her sly smile. Lauryn looked at him and simply smiled because, after more than five years of him controlling her, it was finally coming to an end. Nottage told her that she had made their job quite easy because she'd had sense enough to open the line by dialing 919. She had her father to thank for that; he always told her that if she got in a situation where she was being attacked, just dial 919.

The Magistrate called the court to order. Kenyon listened as they played the tape. All he wanted to do was get up and kick Shannon's ass around. What was really upsetting him was that Shannon kept looking at Lauryn and smiling. A few times Lauryn looked up and simply smiled at him, and for a split second, his anger disappeared. It didn't take long for the Magistrate to sentence Shannon; she sentenced him to twenty years because this was his first arrest.

When Lauryn heard how much time he got, she felt like the Magistrate was more than fair. She also felt like that chapter in her life was closed.

When she got outside the courthouse, she took a deep breath, and her mind started to go to a million different places. Even though she felt closure, she knew she would have to face Shannon one more time.

Max looked over at his daughter, who was a carbon copy of his beloved wife of more than twenty-five years. He could tell she had something on her mind. She had the same expression her mother had when something was on her mind.

"What are you thinking about, Rae?"

"Daddy, can you take me over to the prisoner dock? I want to speak with Shannon."

Max wanted to say no, but he could see in her eyes that she needed to tell him whatever was on her mind for closure.

"Sure, baby girl, anything you need for some closure."

Max was able to convince Jonathan and Kenyon it was okay to leave Lauryn's side and go home with Angelica. He needed to take Lauryn for a drive before bringing her home. At first they both told them they would go with them, but Max said no.

Jonathan looked at Lauryn, then looked over to the prisoner dock. He shook his head. He understood why his other half was making sure she got closure in this chapter.

Max helped Lauryn over to the dock. Lauryn kissed her father and told him, "I have to do this on my own, Daddy." Max nodded; he completely understood.

When Lauryn got to the dock, Nottage and Wells were the officers who accompanied her. Lauryn looked at them and smiled before looking over at Shannon, who was being brought in by two other officers. His hands were cuffed to both sides of the chair where he sat.

Nottage assisted Lauryn to the chair, then looked over at Shannon. "Be very careful; we will be watching your smart ass." Then he said to Lauryn, "We will stand right outside if you need us."

Wells and Nottage left the room and closed the door behind them. Lauryn felt comfortable because she could see both Wells and Nottage, her new guardian angels.

Shannon gave her a sly smile. "So, are you coming to tell me that you made a mistake?"

Lauryn just looked at him and shook her head. "No, I didn't, Shannon, but I did come to tell you that I feel sorry for you. You're a troubled boy; not a man, but a boy. I pray that one day you actually feel some remorse for what you did to me. I personally don't think you are all bad; I just think you are hurting, and you're a scared little boy who doesn't want to be like this father, but ended up just like him. Shannon, I pray that God blesses you and keeps you."

Lauryn looked over at the man she had allowed to control her life for more than five years and saw nothing but a boy. She truly prayed that he got the help he needed because Shannon was not all that bad; he was just hurt.

When she came out of the prisoner dock, she felt like she had been reborn; like the Lauryn who could take on the world.

Chapter 23

Later that afternoon, Lauryn, Mia, Renée, Lena, and Angelica were all sitting around the kitchen table, laughing and talking, while the men were out on the porch playing dominoes.

Angelica was cutting a slice of guava cheesecake for the now very pregnant Lena. "Thank you, Gigi," she happily said, digging into her dessert. The ladies laughed at Lena as her face lit up like it was Christmas morning.

"Lena, slow down. The cheesecake is not going anywhere," Lauryn said, trying to steal a piece. Lena playfully hit her hand and went back to eating.

"Rae, please leave your sister alone. When Kenyon gets your little ass pregnant, you are going to be around here making demands, as well," Angelica said.

"He won't be getting me pregnant if he doesn't put a ring on my finger," Lauryn said, pointing to her ring finger on her left hand.

"Well, in that case, you need to start picking out the colors, then," Lena said.

"Girl, please shut up. You know he is going to ask you to marry him," Mia said.

"The only question is when," Renée said.

Lauryn looked around the table and started laughing. She couldn't believe they were already planning her wedding, as if Kenyon already asked the question.

"All I have to say is, 'Y'all need to stop talking to yourselves.'"

✳✳✳

Kenyon took a deep breath, as he was about to ask Maxwell Smith for his one and only daughter's hand in marriage. He talked to both his grandfather and his father about his plans. They both told him that marriage should not be taken lightly, and that it was a full time job, but Kenyon was up for the task; he loved Lauryn.

"Max, I love your daughter more than life itself, and I would like to ask you for her hand in marriage. I would do everything in my power to protect, cherish and, most of all, make sure she is always happy."

Max didn't have to think twice about it; he knew for a fact that Kenyon loved his princess. "You can have her hand in marriage." He smiled and gave him a hug.

"Thank you, Daddy," Kenyon said.

Kenyon walked into the kitchen where the women were gathered. He went over to her and kissed her lightly on her lips, then took a spoonful of her cheesecake. Lauryn grabbed the spoon from him. "Get your own, Kenyon."

"I don't want my own when I have yours, thank you very much. Excuse us ladies, but Rae and I are going for a drive." Kenyon said as he picked her up from the table and carried her outside to his truck. To his surprise, she didn't protest.

Lauryn didn't think she would ever get tired of him because she loved him so much, but the journalist in her started to kick in. "Baby, where are we going?"

"Do you trust me?" he asked, not taking his eyes off the road.

"Yes, I do trust you."

"Good."

Kenyon was so nervous. He was able to talk with their old primary school teacher, Mrs. Munroe, who taught them in the fourth grade. When he told her he was planning on asking Lauryn to marry him, Mrs. Munroe gave him the brilliant idea that he should propose to her on their old playground. Once she placed the idea in his mind, it was in a world of its own, especially once he told their families about his plans. He glanced over at Lauryn and smiled, saying a silent prayer for their future.

Lauryn was wondering where they were going when she noticed that they were heading in the direction of their former primary school. She hadn't been to St. Dominic's in forever. The last time she had been there was probably around three years ago when she, Mia, and Renée decide to pay their old teacher, Mrs. Munroe, a visit. She always loved Mrs. Munroe, and it always hurt Lauryn that she would never have children of own.

"Kenyon, why are we here?" Lauryn asked softly.

Kenyon did not say anything as he leaned over and gave her a soft kiss on her lips, then assisted her out of the truck. Kenyon loved holding Lauryn in his arms.

She was getting annoyed because Kenyon would not answer her. Lauryn was trying to figure out why they were at St. Dominic's at six in the evening.

"Kenyon Robert Carter, answer my damn question now," she angrily demanded.

He stopped laughing and kissed her. "Lauryn Rae Smith, to answer your question, the reason we are here is because I feel like playing on the playground."

"Okay," she said.

Kenyon loved when she pouted like a girl; he thought it was cute. He remembered how much she loved to play on the swing when they were in school.

Lauryn felt him pushing her slowly. She closed her eyes and imagined Kenyon waiting for her at the end of the altar, and him coaching her during the delivery of their children. Kenyon glanced down at Lauryn and could tell that she was in deep thought; he watched for a few minutes, realizing that he loved her more than life itself.

He leaned down and kissed her on the cheek. "What are you thinking about, Beauty?"

"I'm thinking about our future."

"What about our future?"

"The part where we get married and we have a house full of children who will drive us to drink," she said, laughing.

Kenyon moved in front of her and got down on one knee. "Beauty, I have been in love with you since we were in the fourth grade, I knew from that night I kissed you that you were going to be my wife, and the mother of my children. Will you do me the honor and make me the happiest man alive? Lauryn Rae Smith, will you marry me?"

Kenyon pulled out a black ring box and opened it. Lauryn was lost for words when she saw the four karat princess cut white gold diamond ring.

"Yes! Yes! I will marry you, Kenyon!" she exclaimed as tears flowed down her face. "I love you, baby."

Kenyon kissed her and placed the ring on her finger. "I love you too, Beauty."

"Kenyon, baby, you know what this means, right?"

"What does it mean, baby?"

Lauryn started playing with his shirt. "This means I only have two months to plan my damn wedding and find my dream home; I want to be a fall bride. Also, we have to get ready for the World Games and the Olympics."

Kenyon just smiled at the woman he was going to marry and said, "Well, Mrs. Lauryn Rae Smith-Carter, whatever you want, your wish is my command. Yes, we have to get ready for the World Games and the Olympics."

"To make history!" they said in unison. They both laughed together.

"I love you, Kenyon."

"I love you too, Lauryn"

Epilogue

Lauryn was at the 200 meters mark doing her warm-up a day after she set the Olympic record in the 100 meters at 10.50 seconds, which had previously been held by American Gold medalist, the late Florence Griffith-Joyner.

Lauryn smiled as she thought about how much her life had changed over the last three years. She first stopped running track, which was her first love, and then let go of all the anger she had towards Shannon, who controlled much of her life. Then she allowed Kenyon to come into her life, and he taught her how to trust again. He also helped her rediscover the real Lauryn.

Kenyon was a man of his word and gave her a fall wedding. She also got her dream home thanks to Kenyon's father, who made sure he put some money up and bought a nice piece of property not far from Lauryn's parents' home. Of course it didn't go over too well with Max being the Commissioner of Police. In reality, the property hadn't been purchased with drug money, but it had been his grandfather who bought the property right before he died.

Lauryn was also keeping a big secret from her husband: that she was twelve weeks pregnant. Only her mother and mother-in-law knew. With all the morning sickness she had been having, she was shocked he hadn't noticed. Lauryn could attest that her husband noticed everything about her.

As Kenyon looked on from the stands, he simply said, "Thank you, Lord, for my wife and my unborn child." He knew she was pregnant, but was just waiting for her to say something. He laughed to himself, wondering why his wife was trying to fool him. He didn't care what anyone said. Lauryn hadn't had a monthly for awhile. Besides, she was getting thick, but he wasn't going to tell her that. Kenyon started to think about how much he had to be thankful for in the last three years. He fell in love with the woman of his dreams, and he finally filled his dreams of winning a gold medal at both the World Games and the Olympics.

Kenyon moved to the end of his seat as the announcer called Lauryn's name. The crowd cheered for her, especially their family and friends who had made the trip to Sydney.

Lauryn wasn't surprised that she had been placed in lane one. Tiffany-Marie Jackson, a runner from the United States, and Kim Ross, her rival from Jamaica, were placed in lanes two and three.

Lauryn waved, smiled, and looked up in the stands when they called her name. She got in position and took a deep breath while listening for the gun. Once she heard it, she left the box perfectly and made her way around the curve, noticing Tiffany-Marie Jackson and Kim Ross-Gordon were neck and neck with her.

That's when Lauryn kicked it into high gear for the last 50 yards. Lauryn knew for sure that she had broken Florence Griffith Joyner's record in 200 meters, also.

She got down on her knees, thanking God for all of his blessings as the official came over and gave her the Bahamian flag, along with Kim and Tiffany-Marie, who both gave her their congratulations.

The announcer called the official results: as Lauryn had won the gold, beating Florence Griffith-Joyner's record time of 21.30.

Tiffany-Marie Jackson won silver, while Kim Ross-Gordon won Bronze.

One of the officials guided her over to the reporters as she was looking around for her husband.

"Can someone please get my husband?" she asked. The official nodded and fulfilled her request.

"Lauryn, how does it feel to break both of Florence Griffith-Joyner's records in 100 and 200 meters? A female reporter asked her.

"I am overwhelmed, happy, and filled with a thousand other emotions all at once," she said with a huge smile.

Lauryn answered a few more questions, when she looked up, she saw Kenyon standing there with his arms wide open. She ran into her husband's embrace and kissed him while placing his hand on her stomach. "I'm pregnant."

Kenyon kissed her again and said with a huge smile, "I know, baby."

Lauryn was not surprised that he knew. "I love you, Mr. Carter."

"I love you too, Mrs. Smith-Carter."

And they both said, "Love on the track!"

Author Bio

I'm Alithea-Jae a DIVA with a Pen! I live in the beautiful islands of the Bahamas. I'm currently a sophomore at the College of Bahamas studying a degree in Media Journalism. I'm actively involved in my community as well as an Advisor for Junior Achievement Bahamas. Writing has always been my first love. I still can remember being put in timeout from my mom for writing on my bedroom wall. After that, she give me a pen and notepad. I have been writing even since. My first novel "Love on Track" will be published in the near future.

Alithea-Jae Lounge(Facebook Page):
https://www.facebook.com/AltheaJae/?fref=ts

Available Now!!!

Mika Windsor's life was slowing becoming perfect. From her new job to her man, everything was falling into place for her; until her ex suddenly pops back into the picture. She tries to avoid him, but when constant reminders of their relationship continues to haunt her, she starts to question everything about her life and her future.

Devin Myers had made a few mistakes in his past, but the one thing he has always had hope in was his relationship with Mika. She was the love of his life and despite all of the obstacles the two has faced, he knew they were destined to be together. While serving time in prison, he planned to reclaim everything that he has lost, including Mika. When an opportunity came to him, he figured that was the perfect moment to get his girl back; but will it be too late?

Anthony Harper has been Mika's new man for almost two years and he loves her unconditionally. But as skeletons began to slowly come out of his closet, Anthony doesn't know what to do, which can ultimately affect his relationship with Mika. Will he be able to cover up his betrayal or will it all come crashing down? Find out what happens when three lives are forever changed in I'm The Only One You Need.

Available Now!!

Sasha is a straight-laced, by the book, plain Jane type of woman. She has walked the path less traveled her entire life and where has it taken her? Nowhere! Sasha decides to forget about her boring life and reconnect with her high school friend Leah for just one night!

I mean seriously. what's the worse that can happen; it's ONE NIGHT ONLY..........

Available July 12th!!

Andrea "Andie" Williams and Dexter Robinson have known each other since they were in diapers. While their parents are the best of friends, the two are barely even acquaintances. While Dexter is the most popular guy at Williamson High School and only cares about which girl he will sleep with next, Andrea is focused on getting into her dream college, Yale.

When they are placed together for an unlikely project, the two have to come together not only to pass their class, but also graduate. With a series of events surrounding them, they both realize that their first experience at love could be with the person who was right in front of them all along.

Stay Connected With SBinkley Publishing

Website: www.sbinkleypublishing@weebly.com

Facebook:
https://www.facebook.com/sbinkleypublishing/?fref=ts

Facebook Group:
https://www.facebook.com/groups/641529035994074/

Newsletter: http://eepurl.com/bY22E9

Made in the USA
Charleston, SC
17 July 2016